Shit Happens!

Desi Boy in America

Author Karan Puri did his schooling from Modern School, Barakhamba Road, Delhi, and went to pursue his Bachelors in Economics from the University of Rochester, New York. He interned in a reputed bank in New York before coming back and doing his MBA from the prestigious International Management Institute (IMI), Delhi. He is an avid reader, writes a blog and this is his first novel. Apart from his job in the corporate world, Karan also aspires to be a freelance writer for various publications.

2nd Edition 2012

Published by
Prakash Books India Pvt. Ltd.
113/A, Darya Ganj,
New Delhi-110 002
Tel: (011) 2324 7062 – 65, Fax: (011) 2324 6975
Email: info@prakashbooks.com/sales@prakashbooks.com

ISBN: 978 81 7234 389 7

Processed & printed in India at Thomson Press

Shit Happens!

Desi Boy in America

KARAN PURI

PRAKASH BOOKS

ACKNOWLEDGEMENTS

I am deeply grateful to my editors Sankalp, Sonalini and Subhojit for going over the manuscript with a keen eye and making helpful suggestions. To Shikha Sabharwal, my publisher, for giving me such a warm introduction to the publishing world.

I will always be indebted to my parents for their unquestioning faith and for letting me go wherever my inclination led. My father who has always been my idol and the one from whom I have learnt the most about life. My mother, for her love and care. My sister who has always been my support. My grandparents, for blessing me from above.

I can never thank my wife enough for believing in me so completely, for allowing me to give more time to my laptop than to her most legitimate demands and yet not frowning in providing me her support and giving me constant feedback on the chapters and putting a meaning behind everything I wrote.

And, finally, a heartfelt thanks to my dear friends from college without whom my college life would not have been so interesting. A special thanks to all Modernite friends for being there for me all through.

Dedicated to my parents

CONTENTS

PROLOGUE

For the first time in over 15 years, the constant buzzing had failed to do its job. Because today, he was up before it could start with its job.

He had heard from friends that these days you get alarm clocks that do all kinds of tricks. Heck, one of them even rolls over and creates a shenanigan from under the bed. Guaranteed to wake you up. Even alarm clocks come with guarantees these days.

But he had preferred the old Titan box clock, with the smooth top buzzer, the plastic depth lines now having become plain over time. This little one had been his friend for years. And one does not replace friends. Not as long as they were alive at least.

And so for the last 15 years, this alarm clock had skillfully done its work without fail. But not today. Because he was already wide awake. Living his dream. Literally.

Anurag Sinha, a West Delhi 21 year old with average build and average features, who had been touted as a nerd all through school, who had been labeled a teacher's pet and had been ridiculed, and ridiculed and ridiculed some more, who had never scored even one point at basketball, who had never been included in hand cricket during recess, all because he was not the type, had now been conferred upon the prestigious title of *The Mastermind*. Anurag Sinha, to put it simply, had done the impossible.

Not that he had thick glasses. He was no Dilton Doiley. Never could be. Did not have *that* tenacity. But he was the best at everything that required brains. And that was finally paying off today.

How many times has it happened to us? Of coming to know about how your neighbor's cousin's sister-in-law's husband's brother got a scholarship to go abroad? And one thought would cross all our minds in unison on hearing this piece of news — *lucky bastard!*

And today Anurag was that neighbor's cousin's sister-in-law's husband's brother!

This had always been his dream. What the hell, this has always been everyone's dream. Gate crashing straight into the big league from a humble, decent, West Delhi existence. Maybe they would do a feature on him in *Time* magazine later sometime. Dreams were meant to be big. And limitless. Aren't they?

Anurag had been sitting in bed all through the night.

Around two in the morning, he'd given up his losing battle with wide-eyed insomnia and propped himself up on the bed stand. Pillow on his lap, his future in his eyes, he could almost taste tomorrow.

This was going to be some sort of a first-time for him. Like a virgin. Indira Gandhi International Airport. Immigrations. Customs. Passport. He did not even understand much of it. He was so scared of what was going to happen to him at the airport that the thought of being deported too crossed his mind. *Wasn't it a term used with immigrations? What did it do? Oh God!*

All his bags were packed, he was ready to go. And as he kept sitting on his bed, his bulbous eyes searching through the darkness, the silence being evenly distributed by the tick-tock of his old friend, all he could think of was the years that had led him on to this gargantuan moment in his life.

The Reason

It had all started with the accelerator of a Bajaj Chetak, at the time when it was prestigiously and affectionately called "Hamara Bajaj", jingle and all included. It happened quite some many years from today — when bell bottoms were the most *in* thing in fashion and even men took pride in wearing floral full sleeved shirts.

Ridge Road in Delhi at that time remained lifeless for the major portion of the day. It still remains lifeless for the major portion of the day? *Alright, so some things never change.* And it was on this very Ridge that the germ of Anurag's life was sown when at three o' clock on the 18th of October, 1975, Mr. Varun Sinha took the love of his life, Ms Devika Sharma, for a joyride.

As the Chetak sped down one of the many slopes, Devika suddenly realized that they were gaining speed. First it was the "fun" speed, and then it started tilting towards the "crazy" speed, until the time when it finally reached the "numbing" speed.

With strands of her hair leaping out of the helmet and zig-zagging across her face, Devika first experienced fear. She tried to whisper into Varun's ears to slow down, but she could almost hear her small little words dash out behind her and being left like the trail of Hansel and Gretel's bread crumbs.

She readjusted her vocal chords and yelled into the wind, and even though Varun heard, he refused to slow down. Rather, the scooter just kept gaining more and more momentum. It was a death ride. Devika kept screaming and screaming, while Varun kept speeding and speeding.

And then he spoke for the first time that day, on that ride, on Ridge Road.

"Either you marry me, or I keep speeding. What will it be?"

Fear turned to surprise, then to shock, to awe, and finally, to laughter. All this, for *this*! She loved her man. Her man was a funny man. He was also quite brilliant. And there was only one response you could give to a funny, brilliant man you loved.

"Yes."

And the scooter came to a screeching halt, burning rubber.

And the result of this: Anurag Sinha. He got his father's brains and the darker side of his mother's good looks. Consequently, he ended up being a brainy but an average-looking kid. Sadly, brains can never be seen externally. And even if they could, how on earth would it help? Anurag would still have been an average looker with a standard brain. No one would have known what awesome stuff lay inside that brain!

But one thing was there for sure, Anurag suffered from persecution all through his life. He never could really dream big. As far as he was concerned, he just never thought he had it in himself to do anything, right or wrong. And that stuck with him for a long, long time. Perhaps even till his date with darkness that night.

And nothing was ever normal for him. Everything happened to him for a self-ascribed reason and the reason was always bad. He started school under the impression that his parents sent him there because he fought with his cousins, or played with the local stray dog — or could it be that one time when he had tried on his father's underwear? *How did they ever know?*

But barring the fact that he had only a handful of friends, Anurag's college days went along just fine. As in, not as fine as he had hoped they would be, but fine enough as far as his study program was concerned. He was the guy who got straight A's, he was the one who always got picked by teachers to answer tough questions, and he was the one who always had the answers to every single question.

Teachers loved him, the back-benchers hated him.

All right, not every teacher loved him. How could they? Particularly the ones who were in charge of physical education? Sure, he scored the highest marks in theory, but he was always a hair space away from failing practicals. Whether they passed him because they felt sorry for him, or whether they passed him so that they wouldn't have anything to do with him, this mystery will perhaps never get solved.

But even though the education system under which he studied was textbook-oriented and Anurag never had a problem with textbooks, Anurag was not happy. Because mostly everyone in school, in his class, on the campus, had a girlfriend whereas he did not.

There were ugly girls, average girls, pretty girls, and extremely pretty girls all around him. Except for perhaps uglier than ugly ones, they were all out of his league. Not that he could do any better either. He may have been well read and known every question in class, but someone should have heard him talking to girls. *Riot!*

This one particular incidence is the most famous of all. It is considered historical by one and all in the school. Some students go to the extent of deeming it as historical as the school's foundation. It happened one dark and windy day, during the recess.

Alisha Mahapatra, the sexiest and the dumbest girl in class, was having trouble completing her trigonometry homework. Her boyfriend Amit, the school cricket team captain, was dumber than her. He was a freaking Greek God, but he had the brains of a monkey lemur. Let alone together, even if they had taken the help of the entire cricket team, they could have never come anywhere close to completing the given set of problems. They could think of only one way out of the problem. Anurag.

Alisha, with her dumb brains and pretty head, decided that the easiest way to get Anurag to lower his code of discipline and honesty and to get the job done was to seduce him. And so, during recess that day, when the sun was nowhere to be seen and the skies were ready to cry at the tragedy to unfold, she walked up to Anurag, who was sitting and eating all by himself on one of the metal benches in the playground, and suddenly jumped in front of him making sure that her breasts were shoved right in his face.

A rattled Anurag's reflex pushed Alisha back with all his might, making her tumble to the ground and without stopping, he picked up his tiffin box of mucky sandwiches and tomato ketchup and threw it all on her to make sure that whatever it was that had attacked him stayed down.

Poor Alisha. Covered in red and sticky ketchup, with soggy tomato pieces jammed all over her beautiful tresses. And the backdrop — an entire cricket team coming after Anurag. No one got trigonometry done. But Anurag got done very well.

He was whacked all through the recess- bruised, punched, battered, kicked. He was in such a daze with the way events had tumbled around him in that short time that even his tears froze and he became a wreck.

And even though the recess eventually got over and with it his beating, the moment became engraved in everyone's minds for life. When Anurag came to school the next day, there was not one eye that looked anywhere but at him. And though he turned away and he tried to look down away from them, he could still see them sniggering.

And thereafter Anurag was on some kind of a marked-list. Marked for bullying. Marked for ridicule. Life in school before this had been fine enough for him, nothing hunky-dory, but nor too bad either. But after the incident the process of humiliation that ensued grew slowly but steadily, forcing Anurag to retreat into his shell deeper and deeper.

When it all became too much to bear, Anurag made a pact with himself. A silent pact with the soul, the most important of all pacts that he made in his life. He resolved that would prove them all wrong. He would do something the idiots around him will never be able to do. It took many checks and balances inside his head before he could narrow down his revenge proposals. After all, it had to be something unique. Something that no other could achieve. Something humanly impossible!

It was then that it struck him; the best way for him to show them that he was not lesser but better than them was to get a scholarship to go and study abroad in the US of A. In *The place*. And he would do it. Amit would never be able to play in the Indian national cricket team. Alisha would never become Miss Universe. But he, Anurag Sinha, would go abroad and study. Would get a foreign degree. Would let them know that he can do something as great as that while they can only be losers, mere hapless bystanders.

And the day had come when he was standing at that very crossroad of his life, when he was all set to go to the USA to study. At University of Rochester, one of the finest universities in the world, a university that people would kill to get into, may even sell their kidneys and give away their colons for free in the deal. He was going to such a place. To study Masters in Economics.

But today, as he sat trivializing his past and picturing his future in the void between the life that had been and the life that was going to be, everything seemed childish to him. He had no idea what Alisha or Amit were doing after so many years. Where they were, what they were up to, whether they were alive or dead even. And the fact that he was going to the US, having beaten off thousands of co-applicants to get the coveted seat in the prestigious college was far too great to be just a revenge motif, he thought.

But let's keep the thoughts away for now because Anurag Sinha, the man, is all set. As the first rays of the day are breaking in, he is sitting on his bed, waiting for the alarm to ring. A trusted friend will signal the start. Once again.

Going Away

Whatever happened in Anurag's household happened with a little greater intensity than other Delhi households. So, when it was known that the son of the house is going to leave for America in a couple of weeks, Sinha Nivas became hysterical.

First of all not only the whole family, but also the entire neighborhood, even the *doodhwalla* came to bid Anurag farewell. The kinswomen found themselves unable to hide their tears on seeing Anurag. Overlapping tales starting from the time Anurag was delivered by a grotesque looking nurse and ending in the present were recited by everyone. Mrs. Devika Sinha always led the pack in this field, and added a greater plethora of femininity in the stories than the other women.

But the Sinha men were different. When the sun set on the eve of Anurag's departure, they ripped into their

Johnny Walkers to celebrate. Varun Sinha, the proud father, being the host, led the pack in this case, Many brand new bottle of branded alcohol were opened and many *patiala* toasts were raised to the son's success.

And poor Anurag! In this whole melee, he had to shuffle between one section of the house and the other. While in the female section, he had to quiet the weeping females, especially his mother, that all would be fine and he would not have any trouble in eating American junk food as opposed to her home cooked greasy *aloo paranthas*, and he would have to rush back to assure his drunk father that he would not lose out on the dating business because he was an Indian.

Naturally, that was a drunk father talking.

After several pegs of free Johnny Walker had been settled down in their pot belly, Anurag's uncles would also come and offer fair amounts of business advice to Anurag.

"Beta, what will you do after your studies are over? Have you thought about that?" his uncle Suresh came and questioned.

"No Chacha, right now I am only looking forward to life in America!"

"Ah, but beta, future is future. You think about future and you go places. Else you stay in present," came the rehearsed answer.

Anurag kept wondering why his Uncle, who had never made it beyond the eighth grade and had then gone on to start a small sale hinge factory, was somehow adamant about speaking to him in English that day.

Anurag shared this weird feeling with Deepak, his chacha's son. "He thinks he has to speak to you in English since you are going to America. Asshole!" Deepak said.

Deepak was the only person in the family with whom Anurag could really be himself. The Sinha men of the generation before them had seldom completed their education, even though they had brains, before branching off into what they called '*bijinesh*', but they made sure that the present generation went through the whole package of school, bachelors and post-graduation.

And the present generation appreciated this concern. After all the only responsibility that college offered them was to get good marks. They did not have to think about the bacon as long as they were still in some educational institution learning how to make a lot of bacon later on in life.

Deepak and Anurag were both in the same boat. The others in line were much younger.

"So," Deepak began, drunk clandestinely on some pegs, "how'll you handle the girls in America?"

"Don't know! I guess I'll figure it out once I get used to the place."

"Come on, it's not like we are in the 1970s! America is no longer an alien country. Why, we are more American these days than the American themselves," Deepak argued.

"Yes, I agree… But then, think about it. It might still take me quite some time to get used to some things, for instance the accent, what if I am made fun because of my accent."

"Big deal! See, 'big deal'… I'm sure that expression originated in Vishnu Sharma's *Panchatantra*! Anyways, it's easy to ape the American accent, just slant your vowels and shorten the consonants, and you'll do just fine!"

"Hmmm…Boy! I can't believe it's finally time!"

"Yup! I think you should start getting ready to leave. Your father is gesturing towards a new bottle."

Three Toyata Innovas full of people started off towards IGI an hour later. The men at the wheels were drunk and the women were still recalling odd passages of history nostalgically. It seemed to be the longest drive of Anurag's life. But it was just the beginning. Things got worse at the Terminal building when even the men started crying, but, naturally, in their own manly way. As it turned out, one of the Innovas was carrying a big orange garland that was thrown over Anurag, whose face garbed itself in clothes of disbelief, embarrassment and horror, even as Deepak kept giggling at his predicament.

Soon, some cops came and broke up the clamorous assembly citing traffic snarls and Anurag was finally left in some peace. But then Devika started murmuring that someone should at least go with her baby inside and make sure that he reached the gate safely and also, if possible, leave him all the way to the plane, to make sure his seat and tray were in their standard upright position or not. This by the way was not possible because of security reasons.

But, Anurag ignored the murmurs, quickly shouted his goodbyes and fled inside.

Anurag had never come into the international section of the airport. The maximum that he had ever done was catch a flight to Kathmandu during their seventh grade annual summer break. But they had flown IA, and had used the Domestic wing of the IGIA.

He carefully went through each and every process: security, check-in, customs, Immigration, etc.

As an anxious Anurag waited for his row to be called in by the Lufthansa staff, he could neither stop his knees from knocking against each other nor keep his fingers from trembling. There was a heavy flow of foreigners in the premises and just the sight of the white women gave him blisters that were both painful and pleasurable, internally.

Deepak was right. How would I ever talk to women there?!

Finally, the time of flight arrived. Anurag sat strapped in the huge flying cigar that was to take him to New York with a layover at Frankfurt for some hours. He had got a window seat. But as it turned out the other two seats in his row had been bought by two very pretty women. Foreigners. White.

Orientation had begun.

Sounds of Silence

Anurag's father was a unique figure, he was an alcoholic and had often shamelessly counseled his only son about the benefits of drinking. In fact, ever since Anurag's 18th birthday, he had been hell-bent on opening his son's eyes to the unparalleled joys of drinking.

Anurag's father would have loved to have his son with him on a breezy warm afternoon and down a few beers. Varun wanted every chance to slip into gear now that his son *was* 18.

But Anurag was not sure. He never was sure about stuff like that. Alcohol in Anurag's school books was always associated with immorality and he wouldn't touch it. Not even when he was offered a glass by his very own blood father.

But today, a few thousand feet up in the sky, sitting next to two blondes all anxious and excited about the new phase that life was going to usher, his father's words started ringing in his head.

It soothes your nerves, gives you peace, allows you to think better. Don't you see why Americans always have a drink before doing anything… And look where they have gone. The trick, my son, is to drink and not get drunk!

Over and over, like the air hostess' repeated instructions about metal seat belt clasps and oxygen inhalers, these words kept going through Anurag's head. He needed strength. Strength to even fall asleep next to these two girls. And the niggling thought of what it would be like for him in America if he could not even get by two women sitting next to him on a flight tore through his insides.

And his delusions increased manifold when the air hostess walked up to him as they were flying somewhere over Kabul and asked him whether he would like a drink. The sixty seconds that followed were one of the most embarrassing seconds of his life: he fumbled, stammered and looked confused and under confident, right before the airhostess and next to the two sexy blondes.

But he finally did it. Unable to think of anything else, he said, 'Scotch,' and the airhostess left him with a mini and a glass filled with ice. Anurag kept staring at it forever. Finally with greasy, sweaty fingers, he finally managed to slip the top off and poured the contents into his glass. And as he lifted his drink, a warm uneasy sensation burned through him. *What if I pass out? Wouldn't I be embarrassing myself further before these women?*

And true. The first cut is always the deepest. And it burned. Like hell. Right through his insides. And even as he subjected himself to such torture, the only thought that run through his mind was why do grown up, respectable people torture themselves willfully like this every time they have a drink.

Even as he bore the pain with a straight face, twitching his nose and biting his lips so as to not scream, all he could think of was how the women next to him seemed so satisfied after having taken mammoth sips out of their own glasses filled with alcohol. *Man, western women are really something!*

And then it became worse. The burning sensation inside gave him an urge to puke. But he would have to go to the loo to get rid of the urge. And in order to go to the loo, he would have to ask the two blondes to shift and give him space to pass by!

What if I just try to keep sitting and try to shift my focus from the urge? No! You never know what could happen and I am not the one for finding out.

The whole game had now gone to level two. First, it was terribly inconvenient for him to open his mouth as that made the puking sensation worse. And second, he had no choice but to ask the ladies for space to go to the passage. Double whammy!

He couldn't get through either level, he knew that, the odds were weighed down real heavy against him. As he tried to work a way out of the prevailing predicament, his stomach rumbled and suddenly he also started feeling the urge to shit. Soon his whole ass started burning. It was the most terribly discomforting experience of his whole life.

He just had to make a move now. He simply had to. There was no other way out of the mess. What could he do? What *would* he do?

He shifted for a few seconds in his own seat and then decided to make a move. He crouched up and as he turned to look at the women, his misery increased. He had earlier hoped to simply smile and hold out his hand towards the leg space. That would have been enough.

But now it was different. The whole semantics had changed. As he turned his head to deploy his plan and achieve his objective, he was horrified to note that after having washed down their vodkas, the pretty ladies had wrapped themselves in the airline blanket and had cozily nodded off.

He was trapped. On more than one count now. Would it be good manners to wake the sleeping? How loud could he raise his voice? Did etiquette dictate that he could tap their shoulders? What if what he thought were shoulders beneath the blanket actually turned out to be their boobs? Would it tantamount to molestation if he unknowingly tap them? Would they scream? Would he be thrown off the plane and left in a troubled country, say Iraq? Would the Americans in Iraq agree to see his US Visa?

His anxiety did seem a tad bit unjustified. But it was hard. And it was going to be harder for someone like Anurag Sinha who was paranoid of girls.

He had to clear his mind, he had to think. Since there was no physical process to clear one's mind, Anurag decided to clear his throat first. Maybe that'd start a whole domino effect throughout his body.

Lo and behold! The woman sitting right next to him in the aisle seat peeped through one of her eyelids and saw Anurag standing there like a dodo, looking distraught. The site was too amazing and she decided to take a proper look at this weirdo in a half-arched position.

"Need to use the restroom, do ya?" came the obvious question.

Anurag, almost being able to smell victory, carried out his thought-of plan. He flashed all his teeth at her and swept his palm through the walkway, more like a smiling traffic cop signaling the right way to a politician.

As he crept along, trying his very level best not to touch any portion of the blondes but he couldn't pass without brushing his knees against both women's legs, The touch made him feel apologetic, but also drove a sizzling sensation up his spine.

The flight was to last four or so hours more. And, during this time, whenever he would sit, sleep, or stand, there would be two women right next to him. Was it always going to be like this from now on? Would his life center around clearing his throat or sweeping his palms? Was coming to the States a whole bloody mistake that he had willingly made?

No. He had come to the States to study. To get a degree. And if he just put his head down and kept to that, he would not need anything else. If he was not able to make friends, he would do without friends, he knew how one could live without friends.

But, in a foreign land thousands of miles from his place, would he be able to do without friends? Would making friends in the US become a necessity?

Klosett

Walking into Frankfurt airport felt weird. It was like walking right into a James Bond set. Glass panels, swinging doors, never-ending pathways, criss-crossing multitudes– all indifferent to the person standing there staring at them. And then he spotted a mini car turning away from him with an invalid at the back. *A car being driven right inside an airport!* And then he saw more cars and even cycles running inside and was stunned at the spectacle. It was a tad too much for Anurag to swallow.

They had left the shores of the motherland, and it was then, standing in an alien land surrounded by foreigners, that he really understood the term "motherland" all of a sudden. He understood what it meant to be an Indian all of a sudden.

He had left Delhi at 0200 hours, and after a grueling, doubt-ridden eight hour journey, had arrived at Frankfurt at 0700 hours local time. It was well past his usual time to go to the loo, and the mental agony aboard the flight was now making him jump to it even more.

Even though all the signs leading to the restrooms were bilingual, all he could see were the German letterings. Maybe it was a weird kind of hallucination being caused by a sweating bowel.

With great difficulty, and luckily without managing to cause a traffic jam in the middle of the airport, he was finally able to find his way through to the toilet. It seemed as if all planes from all over the world had decided to land at Frankfurt at that very moment. Naturally every person on each and every one of these aircrafts wanted to use the facilities.

At first he thought he'd keep moving from door to door, perhaps hear a flush and know that he would be next. But then everyone started queuing in one single row and as and when a door would open, the first person in the row would enter. Not like back home, people did not queue up outside their own chosen, respective doors. Anurag was not in that row, he was just moving from door to door, confused. People who came after him were leaving before him.

Finally he understood and followed the foreign etiquettes and after quite some time, Lady Luck smiled upon Anurag and opened the door of paradise for him. Not quite Paradise, but at least doors of comfort. A relieved, grateful Anurag rushed in and got to his act immediately. PEACE. In capital letters.

But a crisis happened after attaining *moksha*. Old Indian systems die hard. And 'new' western practices take time to get used to. And it was happening right there, right then, in a small "nose touch the door" area. And it was happening to Anurag. He had forsaken his misfortunes, but his misfortunes had not left him.

All his life, Anurag had used the tried and tested Indian formula of washing one's ass after crapping in the morning. But, today, the main object of that process was missing. Objects actually: water and mug. And it was a dangerous position to be in, at least for Anurag.

And even as he came to grips with the lack of equipment around him, and as he realized the gravity of the situation he was in, harsh reality stared at him in the face. Not that literally, though there was plenty of material to read while sitting on the ceramic throne — graffiti on the walls of autocratic dictators and their proposed fates. But the problem that he came face to face with was that his plane could leave and he would be trapped in this cubicle, even perhaps till the time his visa ran out.

All that he had was toilet paper with him. And there was no way that he was going to use it. He'd much rather sit there, be deported back to India than soil himself with such a heinous crime. Damn, he already was soiled. And defeated. There seemed to be no other solution at hand. This was what it really meant to be trapped. And at the risk of repetition, *defeated*.

There was nothing that he could do except actually

doing it. He had to. All the other solutions that he tried to concoct met with failure. Serious failure. Absolute failure. He would have to adapt. He had to.

And he did. He had to get out of there. He had to go back into the terminal and wait for his flight call. He had to reach the States. New York beckoned. His life beckoned. Anurag gingerly reached out for the wad of toilet paper that had been ceremonially placed besides him and started using it. Disgusted. Disgruntled. He did it. He had to do it.

It took him forever to be free of that niggling doubt that remained behind his back. He just went on pulling paper, after paper, after paper. Luckily for him, the cleaning staff had left an extra roll of paper there. Fate it seemed knew that he was going to come in there. Sufficient preparations had been made. The dye had been cast, and he just had to play his part.

Finally, when even the second roll was over and finished with, and a lot of the same area had been worked upon, though still not certain, though still not confirmed, Anurag knew that there was nothing more that he could do. He had to leave. Leave the rest to fate, and leave his doomed hole in the wall.

Managing to arrange his pants in a manner suitable, so that nothing stuck to nothing and there was hopefully no possibility of a wedgie, he was finally ready to move on. In life, out of the loo.

As he opened the door, and launched his wind up, the next person anxious to start doing his thing went right in.

Anurag knew that the man would start with his business immediately on closing the door, but only when he wound up would he realize that he had no toilet paper to use. Anurag ran the run of his life, hoping this person had not made a mental impression of him.

Thankfully the traffic snarls inside the airport was now worse than ever. The maze had become even tighter and the plentitude of masses would surely cover his tracks from the loo and the abominable act that he had committed. *Who cares as long as I am content. Or am I?*

The Lufthansa flight to New York had already started filling in people into the cabin and the first few sections were already done with. It seemed like an eternity, but after about five minutes, five whole minutes, Anurag and his bunch of merry men were called in by the fat German lady who looked good enough to kill, physically, to board the aircraft.

Anurag gave one last cursory look behind him, to measure the scene of the crime and saying a silent prayer for the man in the loo, Anurag walked into the last leg of his journey. Next stop, New York!

Not Born in the USA

When Anurag slipped into his window seat once again, he was, well, not really surprised to see that seated beside him were the same two women who had accompanied him from Delhi, the same two women who had perhaps gifted him kidney stones. And he wasn't really surprised, because come on, after all it was *him*. Bad things always happened to him and they would keep happening. America was going to be no different and the trip so far had proved that it was not going to be different than life back at home. He would just have to get used to it.

But since he had already mastered the art of withstanding the two women, Anurag thought that the next few hours in the flying cigar would not be as uncomfortable as were the first few between Delhi and Deutschland. But when the amazingly striking blonde next to him fell asleep on his shoulder, Anurag was back to his usual palpitating self, even though he tried to convince himself to enjoy the touch.

And even as the vast blue below them and above them made him feel like Aunt Lata's soggy sandwich, Anurag slowly started to look forward to life in the States to alienate the current trauma. New possibilities, new responsibilities, new classes, new people, new everything. Perhaps things would change. Hopeful at least.

And even as the clouds and the azure blue around him stayed on, the foggy bottom of the horizon soon changed contours to show land. Like Magellan, or for that matter any of the explorers of yore, Anurag felt his stomach button up. Not because of an air pocket, but because he could finally scream "land ahoy!" It was a new sensation. A remarkable sensation. He felt he was Columbus.

And it was not just land. There were buildings too. Huge buildings. Glass buildings. Each one trying to outdo the other. It was like a Hollywood movie in 3D. Only that this time, it was for real. Anurag was as ecstatic as a child flying for the first time on beholding such a show of modern architecture for the first time. It was a time of firsts. Surely. And it was just not a foreign country he could see from above, it was the mother lode of them all. It was the United States of America. The land of dreams, hopes, possibilities. The land of all lands. And he was going to be the first from the Sinha family to set foot and begin his tale there.

And as the landscape became more and more prominent, and the buildings came within handshaking-distance, Anurag begun to forget not only his fears and apprehensions but even his perennial dilemma of karmic penance that had remained his affliction all through life.

The idea of America started assuming the role of an anti-tetanus shot with the first sight, from the flight. This shot was going to cure everything, even act as a preventive measure. It was going to be the start of a new life. A Rebirth.

From that point onwards, Anurag heard and felt every little process that brought him closer to the American soil —the opening of the wheels, the snap of the flaps, the clasping of seat belts, the rustling of dreams. Everything was now within his reach. He felt like a different person just at the sight of US. *Imagine what will happen once I actually land!*

And then finally... touchdown. The gentle screech, and then the humming, the booming acoustics of the large plane slicing through American air and causing cataclysmic friction with the opposing wind, and finally the halt. A dream seen long ago was realized. Even as Alisha and Amit got ready to go to bed in their homes in another part of the world, unknown, unsung, Anurag Sinha had capitalized on their insult.

Though the burly yet attractive German women ordered restraint veiled in requests through the PA, Anurag wanted to shed his docile servitude to the spoken words and break free in true blue Delhi style. He could not wait for the aircraft to come to a perfect halt. He could not wait to open the luggage rack and start digging out his small little bag. He had come too far and had waited too long to tolerate any more delay. Hell, if the aero bridge were to take its own sweet time to fix itself to the door, he'd jump. Right onto America. His arrival will surely create a big splash then.

But this was not India. For all the recession-resistance, India was slow. She wants to move like America, she wants things to function as smoothly, she considers herself better than America, but the truth is a different tale altogether, Anurag thought. Something or the other always messes things up back at home. That will not be here in America.

Anurag had once heard a Bengali saying from his bong friend Girish, *"Korta'r gu-e gondho nei."* Roughly translated, it means, "Boss's shit never stinks". Anurag realized the truth of the saying for the first time that day. At customs.

America may be fast, time may be money, but security comes here even above the President and God, Anurag realized. It was not that the process was slacking, it was just that the entire thing was time consuming. He recalled seeing a few years ago the video footage of Saddam Husain being checked after being nabbed flashing on his television screen. He recalled watching a pair of hands groping his mouth, running its fingers all through his teeth, pulling out his tongue, turning him around and even checking his asshole.

Was the same happening again? To all the people who had got off the flight? Actually, CIA or FBI or whoever the shit was looking into the whole process was making sure that there were no more terrorist attacks and that no more skyscraper fall to the ground like a house of cards. Therefore, the wait was extremely tiring, especially after the Delhi–Frankfurt flight, the Frankfurt-Au-Main restroom fiasco, and the Frankfurt–New York journey, but Anurag felt safer here. Much safer than he had ever felt at home.

When he finally moved to a kiosk, with a striking police officer in black offering him a practiced smile, Anurag was beaming. The officer took his passport and forms and went through them like a well-oiled clock.

"What brings you the United States of America, sir? Business, or pleasure?" One of the many usual questions asked world over by customs officer; only the name of the country remains a variable.

Now this was somewhat of a trick question for Anurag who had taken great care to make sure that he stood in a queue leading to a male cop. Anurag did not distinctly fall under any one category and yet he was not guilty of misusing his visa. He had learnt from Steven Spielberg's *The Terminal* that US security and government staff are rather helpful, particularly the ones at the airport, and therefore he decided to take the aid of the police itself.

"I am here to study, sir… What would that be — business, or pleasure?" Anurag answered his cheekiest answer ever and immediately became quite awed at his own guts. But the feeling evaporated soon, and Anurag was scared shitless yet again: *would he mind my cheekiness?*

But somehow the Customs officer seemed to like it because it brought a smile on his lips. "Well sir, if you plan to study here and go back home, then I'd say pleasure... But if you stay back and take away my job, then I'd call it business. Ain't that a bitch now?"

Now Anurag once again felt that same burning sensation in his ass. The one that he had on the plane. Was the smile flashed at him sarcastic? Was that a threat? *"Leave my country, or else"* kind of a warning. Help!

But a few more routine questions — routine for the Customs officer, not for Anurag — and he was given the standard 'success' quote, "Thank you, sir, and enjoy your stay in America." And that was it. And it was then that it finally hit him. The last barrier between him and the actual, real American soil had been crossed, hurdled, whatever you want to call it. He had arrived, had cleared his literal "entrance exam" and now he was about to step out and feel it, know it, realize it: Anurag Sinha was finally in the United States of America.

The Damned Apple

Anurag had joined the University of Rochester, one of the foremost educational institutions of the country — a place where, to get in, most Indians would happily give away their right and left arms. And perhaps also throw in a leg and a liver. And Anurag had practically sailed in there, a feat achieved only by a very few, handful of people.

He had a day to spend in New York before he'd take the train from Grand Central to Buffalo, from where he would get to *The Flower City*, Rochester, and head for the university. But that was to be the next day. Today was going to be NYC Day, a day in a city which was like the capital of the world for most people including our hero.

Now Anurag had two choices before him: moving into a bed-and-breakfast for the day and then getting into the city, or saving even that money and blowing it all on and around the city. Plus there was also the factor of the luggage. He possibly could not walk around the city lugging the huge suitcases now, could he?

The B&B option seemed better as that would give him space for keeping his suitcases and a bed for the night. But Anurag so wanted a second opinion. He knew that once he is in Rochester, studies and all would take over his life. The window to return to NYC later looked bleak and cloudy. Anurag did not want to be the moron who passed up on New York City because he was sleeping in some shady Bed and Breakfast!

Anurag decided to chuck the B&B option. He walked straight out of the airport and felt the bustle of New York before him, face to face. *Perhaps if I look around I might spot Catherine Zeta Jones step out of her cab!* It was a culmination of his dreams, right there, right at that spot!

Very much *à la The Terminal,* Anurag hailed a cab and gingerly placed himself in it. A huge difference from the usual autos that he was used to back at home. *Here cabs are better than most people's limos back home.* Everything in America seemed better. End of story. Nothing could put down anything of America for Anurag at that point.

The cab driver, a Russian immigrant who had broken free from the chains of opportunist communism back home and had smuggled himself into the by-lanes of New York, asked in a crisp, vodka strained, short syllabled, "Wherrre um ahi takin yo?" And it was at that moment that it actually hit Anurag — he had not just come to America, he had not just come to New York, he would not just be going to Rochester the next day, he had actually come to a global crossroad where he would see people from everywhere converge and pass by him. His cab driver was a Russian, the man across the street might be Polish, Dracula was Scandinavian and he was an Indian. Everyone was there, waiting to turn the meter and get along with their work. *This, is unity in diversity.* No one bothered where you came from as long as the work you did got done on time and got done with accuracy. The rest be damned.

"I would like to go to Grand Central please... The railway station!" Anurag replied to Dmitri Shkel, as his ID card spelt out.

"Naw proablem! You in Aamerica fur da fust time?" *Do Indian auto drivers talk this much with their passengers?*

"Yes, I just landed from India. I'm going to the University of Rochester tomorrow, where I'm going to study Economics. So..." Anurag tried to break a smile, though at that time all he wanted to do was look out of the windows and stare at America whiz by.

Dmitri seemed to pipe down, Anurag realizing that he had to focus on the roads that led out of JFK into New York City. And that fact about America was right. Everyone was in a hurry. The race to the destination was always on and if you could not make it there on time, before everyone else, then you would be perhaps judged. You always needed to be the best at whatever you did in America. There was no place for a second place.

Cabs were converging at a point, ready to split and then

break off into different directions. It was a race: whoever reaches the bottleneck first wins. Dmitri was also a part of this race and, with an experienced hand, he twisted and turned the cab around, so as to fit into even the slightest space that he could find for himself. The battle continued for a while and he somehow reached the freeway and raced towards the tall huge buildings visible in the horizon. Anurag could now see why America was what it was called: B-E-A-U-T-I-F-U-L.

But soon they had to slow down as traffic snarl, which to be very honest were even worse than the ones in Old Delhi, arrived before the huge tall buildings did. Alright, the snarls were organized affairs, but they were traffic jams no less! Dmitri once again tried using his experienced hand to manage his way through. But he did not do it the way auto drivers do in Delhi — it wasn't like he was trying to cross lanes, or worse, stand in between two lanes. He performed all the maneuvering smartly without violating any rules. However, despite his best efforts, they ultimately got stuck and stuck well.

But Anurag did not mind it. He was satiating himself with the moving visuals on his window and the halt did not bother him. Even as his new Russian friend tried steering through the mess further, Anurag kept sitting back in the comfortable seat of the cab, his head pasted on the window, swallowing and digesting every little nuance of the city. He already felt one with everything that was happening around him.

Anurag saw the hot dog stands on the pavements, the ice cream vendors, the florists -- everything here was just the way he had imagined it, just the way he had seen in so many Hindi movies. He in fact felt as if he was a part of some Karan Johar movie. The picture was complete and wonderful. The sights of New York had lived up to every single claim that others had made about them.

It took them another hour from there to reach Grand Central, which Anurag refused to believe was a train station. *It looks like Buckingham Palace*, he thought in the *Delhiwalla* style of calling a structure palatial. Dmitri pulled up his cab beside the curb and a dazed Anurag, while still staring at the terminal building and at his surroundings, hopped off his seat and started pulling his luggage out of the car.

Once he had arranged all his bags on the pavement, while constantly entertaining the niggling thought that someone might come and run away with all of it, a situation which happens all the time in both India and America and also perhaps in every single corner of the earth materialized: as he slumped his head down to check the meter, he saw that it had been wiped clean.

The *Delhiwalla* in Anurag immediately got all riled within. It was the usual trick. Now he would have to fight with this friend-suddenly-turned-foe and make him accept the right fare. But what was the right fare? There was a cop walking down the pavement, coming towards them. *Maybe he can help.* Thinking that a Russian cab driver, who was no doubt illegally working in this country, would be scared shitless of the police, Anurag decided to proceed quickly. He would have to hammer out the truth out of Dmitri before they both lose sight of the policeman.

"How much do I have to pay you?" asked a nervous Anurag, deciding to make his opening statement on a simple mark.

Dmitri bent over sideways to look at Anurag and, with a smile, a smile that Anurag immediately knew was deceptive, replied, "Thiss iss yoar fursst taime inn muy kontry. Thraide wus freeee. Hav ah gudde!"

And then, without another word, Dmitri pulled his cab out of there and got lost in the sea of yellow that dotted the entire road leaving a completely unnerved Anurag standing on the spot. He did not care if the five big black blokes who were standing across the road were to walk over and run away with his bags. He did not care if someone were to come and push him in front of the onrush of cars passing by him at supersonic speed. He did not care if the earth were to part at that point sending him down under. All he could do at that moment was to stand there and try to get one more look at Dmitri's face somehow. Locate him in the melee. Google him perhaps?

And then Anurag's face changed color. He turned pale and made the entire collectiveness walking around him wonder whether the Asian man standing at the edge of the pavement were sick. He looked terrible after what all had just happened before him.

After standing there for what seemed like an eternity, but was actually only two minutes, Anurag slowly turned around oblivious of the fact that the group of black men from across the road were staring hard at him, picked up his luggage and moved closer to the entrance of Grand Central.

He was still not sure of what had made him come to Grand Central, but in that roaring sea of humanity, he was lucky to see a sign across the road that read "LOCKERS". He immediately moved into the line of people who were walking towards there, hopefully not all of them going to the lockers. He did not want another instance of Frankfurt there. Luckily, the Locker room managed by this young man branched off to the left and Anurag was the only person who made that turn.

The Americans seemed accustomed and indifferent to this level of convenience that their nation offered to them but Anurag could just marvel at the locker-provision. There were lockers built into the walls, of three kinds — small, medium and large — and an ATM like vending machine present between the two sets of locker columns. Depending on the size of your luggage, you could make your payment for a desired locker size and the key would just jump out of the cache and you were done. Instant storage.

Seeing the number of bags he had and the size of each, Anurag decided on the large ones and pushed in twenty dollars though the cash slot. Out popped the key to locker number 225 and Anurag marched off in pursuit of his locker. Carefully arranging his bags in, Anurag shut the heavy metal door and turned the key. His bags were taken care of and there was no way in which he could have found a Bed and Breakfast for twenty dollars anywhere in the city.

It was nearly six in the evening and Anurag did a quick mental math to calculate what time it would be back at home in India. He had sent a text to his father on landing at JFK announcing his safety, but a phone call was required to tell his folks how things were in that large labyrinth.

As soon as he came out of the locker enclosure, Anurag crossed the street and walked into Grand Central. He saw signs which led him to the paid phones. A carefully lined row of amazingly good looking and working telephones hung from the wall. It wasn't like the Indian paid phone service where you have to go and ask the man in charge which phone can be used for STD calls and which ones for ISD ones. All phones had every feature here!

Anurag chose an instrument which was at a safe distance from the two phones that were being used by two guys at that moment. After figuring out how many coins he'd have to insert depending on the calling card he had just bought, Anurag finally dialed the number ingrained into his subconscious.

A ring, another ring, a few rings and finally, "Hello?"

Devika. No one else was ever up at this hour at home. His mother got up almost at daybreak to get things ready, so that when the others woke up no one would be late for school, college or work. Today when she was preparing Varun's breakfast and the lunch that he was to carry to work, her attentions in the kitchen were distracted by phone rings. Not the usual rings, but long rings. An STD call perhaps?

"Ma, Anurag here… Can you hear me?"

"Yes, beta, I can hear you perfectly! You reached properly na beta? There was no trouble anywhere during the journey? Nothing happened anywhere na?" A mother's concern about her son traveling international for the first time.

"Na ma, everything was just fine. I had no trouble anywhere. The flight was ok and I reached all ok. Nothing happened anywhere. It was great fun!"

"That's nice beta! How is America…?" And then she started sobbing. Anurag had expected it. As a matter of fact, he had even silently betted with himself that she wouldn't be able to hold up for more than two sentences. And he had won. Even when she was crying, it was nice to hear her voice. Before he had left, at IGI, he was impatient to run away and put two oceans' distance between them. But now that he was so far away, he realized he missed her. Perhaps a little more than his father, but missed them both nevertheless.

The call continued for a while and got disconnected even before he could tell her that his calling card was about to expire and that he would call them again once he reaches

Rochester the next day and moves into the hostel and gets settled. She kept howling throughout, and though he did feel bad, it also felt nice.

As he put the receiver back on, he realized that the phone station next to him was occupied. By a girl. She too had kept back her phone and was searching for something inside her handbag. Anurag eyes got fixed on her. He had never seen anyone or anything quite like her. He just kept staring, while she kept rummaging through her belongings. This was perhaps the only time he would get to stare. Once her eyes were out of there Anurag was going to start dehydrating like always.

"Studying at Rochester?"

It was like a voice that came out of nowhere. It shook Anurag completely. It appeared to be just a looking show without any audio, but suddenly the rules of the game had changed. Considerably. The girl had spoken. She had made a sound, raised a sentence and all this without even looking at Anurag with her head now almost into her bag.

"Excuse me?" was all that he could come up with.

"Sorry, not that I was trying to listen in on your conversation, but sound does travel, you know…" she continued, raising her head finally after finishing the speech.

Blue eyes, blonde, though apparently not quite like the blonde myths. Her lips were ruby red and it did not seem that there was any lipstick on them. She had the perfect nose, angular, crisp but at the same time not like a hook.

Her body was athletic, and the shirt and skirt that she was draped in indicated contours of perfection. Her legs were undoubtedly the best part of her whole appearance, and just on their sight alone, Anurag became speechless, panicky, breathless even.

His girl-trouble in America had started dangerously. It was not just a girl talking to him, it was a Greek goddess. And she had spoken out of the blue. That was worse as that meant he was not prepared. There was no planning that had gone behind this conversation. Not like in the plane. He might not have had a word ready then, but at least he had a body motion worked out. Here it was completely off.

His first thought was whether he should run straight out of the station and run back to JFK in three minutes time and catch the same flight returning to Delhi in which he had arrived. But considering that it took Dmitri more than an hour to get there in the first place, it did not look like such a wonderful idea. There was no way out. He had to speak.

"Uh... I... just... home..." *That wasn't a sentence. Those weren't even words.*

"Boy, you are one serious case of cat got your tongue! You took all that time to come up with that?" and she laughed. Orgasmically. No wonder people call Americans different from the Brits, Brits never laugh at someone stuttering!

"Uh... no... I... mean..." *Speak damn it, speak!!*

"There you go… that was literally much better… Hi, I'm Lizzy!" and she put out her hand towards him. She was making this even worse now.

"Dizzy, Miss Lizzy?" *Thank you John, Paul, George and Ringo.*

"My, my, my… A Beatles fan? That's nice… We are everywhere, aren't we? But just to be certain, where are you from, coz this happens here quite a lot… India, Pakistan or Sri Lanka?

"India… Delhi… Anurag." Much better. He knew that didn't make much sentence sense, but at least it was not completely devoid of any meaning.

"Nice to meet ya! You going to Rochester to study?"

Oh, would the drudgery and the torture never end! "Yes, to study. Tomorrow."

"Great! Welcome to America and to Rochester. I study musicology there. I am going back there tomorrow. By the way, what are you doing today?"

Help!

Lizzy was not actually Lizzy. It was short for Elizabeth. On feeling that Elizabeth was much too common with Queen Elizabeth, particularly after watching Helen Mirren in *The Queen,* and Shekhar Kapur started making his Elizabeth films. And it was when she was fourteen, that she was going through her father's Beatles collection when she chanced to hear upon "Dizzy Miss Lizzy" from the album *Help,* and that brought about the new improved, shortened version.

And it was just not because it was a good shortener, it was also because the nickname had a musical connotation. She loved music. Ever since she was little. Billy Joel was always her first love, but that had spread. Right through the classics, like Sinatra, to the classical work of Mozart. More Mozart than Beethoven. So all in all, two plus two surely made four in this case.

And now she was his friend. His new friend. His second friend in America. And this new friendship was going to last a longer, much longer time than the first, it seemed. After all, she wouldn't simply turn down her meter and run off into the melee like Dmitri. She was in the same University, she was also taking the train tomorrow. Would now sit with him on the train? Lizzy had come to New York to meet up with some friends, and was now planning to paint the city red. And while she had earlier thought of doing that all by herself, now she had company. And not a crowd.

The minute she heard his stammer-ful story—beginning at IGI, Delhi and ending at Grand Central, NY—she immediately started rattling off a deal. She was single in the city, bored to hop around by herself, and he was single in the city, clueless about where to hang out. So it all added up. She was going to be his guide for the day. And also his guide through Rochester.

As they started to move out of the station, all that was going through Anurag's head was why had Lizzy not panicked and ran away from him like most Delhi girls did!

Why was she so hell bent on sticking along? Why was she so willing to act a guide to a stranger? An alien stranger at that! Were all American girls like this? Was he going to have great trouble in the future?

Once they were on the street, Lizzy suddenly jumped in front of Anurag and said, "Just one more thing… You don't have trouble speaking in English, do ya?"

Anurag was a little flabbergasted. How was he going to provide her with an answer. His tongue was still tied into small compulsive little knots. All the way.

"W…W…Wh….y?" *Oh, wonderful.*

"No reason… Just that you don't seem to be talking a lot. Don't be nervous if you can't speak the language well. You'll surely pick it up here. It happens to everyone. Just don't learn the accent too, you know. It will sound very corny when you go back home, if you go at all, that is!" One thing was sure. She was not being sarcastic about anything. She actually meant every word she said. He shouldn't be concerned about his accent because, like she said, there was nothing to be concerned about in the first place. But even then, she said it with a certain warmth and he liked that.

He knew that his state of talking mumbo jumbo was surely going to continue for a while. Why a while, it may continue for a long, long time even. And it would get really embarrassing. For both of them. And that is when it struck Anurag. Would it be better to tell Lizzy about his predicament, about his problem with girls? Particularly with girls like her. Could she be trusted? Or would she think he was a psycho? She was going to be there around him for as long time, so it would be better to tell her.

But, no, the risk is too great!

By the time he came back to his senses from his long philosophical reverie, he realized that they were at the bus stop. And what he realized after that was even worse. He felt something covering his hand. Something had wrapped them within. And in the pushing and pulling at the bus stop, he wasn't able to decipher what it was. Lizzy was standing front of him, straining her neck out to see if their bus was on the way. And when the bus was just about to arrive, he felt himself being pulled, by the hand.

And only then did it become clear to him. She had enclosed his hand in hers. Perhaps it was the practical thing to do. He was new to this country, she was the only one who knew the way about. But then the only problem in this equation was that she had her hand on his. He was not used to it. He also did not want to get used to it. It just scared him shitless. And even as he kept twisting and turning his fist within, all she did was grab it even tighter.

And just because she had decided to adopt the safety precaution of holding hands, he started getting all sorts of weird ideas in his head. Not him, but was she a psycho? Meaning, who behaved this way with a person who one, has met just twenty minutes back! Holding hands and all? How? Why? Eh?

The bus was more or less empty, and they both got

a place to sit instantly. Lizzy paid for their tickets at the driver's seat, which startled Anurag even more. *These buses do not have conductors! I miss DTC already!*

She pushed him towards the window and took the seat right next to his. There was a little too much touching. Making him very nervous. And it seemed that this nervousness was pretty obvious and evident for as soon as the bus started moving once again, he heard a question right from next to him, "Is everything alright? You seem pale!"

What should he do? How should he tell her? How should he tell her everything and not make the situation even worse for him? But if he went along like this, things were going to get worse by themselves!

"I can't tell you…" *Seriously??*

"What? Why?" was her natural response.

"You will think I am crazy!" *So we're doing this, right?*

"I do think you are a little crazy! So you can tell me…" The smile on her face was a little reassuring. It did not give him the liberty to think about going the whole distance still, but yet, there was some solace in her expression. It was like his whole self was suffering from conflicting emotions at that time. No doubt, this situation greatly overshadowed his last most embarrassing situation of getting beaten up during recess. But then, there are no winners here. Only losers.

"Come on, tell me… you can tell me!" She was persistent.

"Well, it's like this…" How was it that when he was speaking the truth, he did not stammer? *Too many questions!* "It's just that I have never really been good at talking to girls…"

"That's it?" Perhaps now she did think that he is crazy!

"Yes, it's never been my strong suit!" *Look at me go!*

"Well, in which case you don't have a problem! It's just a temporary thing… By this evening you won't have any trouble hooking up with girls!"

"I may not have a problem talking to you by the end of the day. But I know I'll still suck at interacting with girls!" This was the longest he had ever gotten without stammering while talking to a girl.

"Hold it right there… First things first, this is America! You know… You need to lay down your Queen's English jazz. It won't work here coz no one's going to understand a word!" and she laughed. He had never seen anyone laugh like that before. Perhaps, it was because he was seeing a girl laugh properly for the first time. This was something else altogether. It sent ripples all through his body. It was a sensation that he had never felt before.

Long after she had stopped laughing, long after she had gone silent, long after they were out on an arterial road, moving towards the Statue of Liberty, all he could hear above the cacophony around him was that laugh. Rippling, unbound, infectious, it had been the most liberating moment of his life, when she had laughed. He could feel his body heave and fall. He could feel it within him.

And it was a feeling like no other. It was a feeling that he had never felt in his whole life. It had to be it. It had to be the moment he had seen off in movies, had dreamt of in his dreams, had read about in books — the four miraculous letters which allegedly gave life a different shape altogether — LOVE.

He was in love. There could be nothing else to it. He was in love with this girl. He had never been in love with anyone before. He knew that he had a problem with girls and he had always left it at that. But, with her, it was all so completely different. He felt so nice when he was with her. And 'nice' was the word he was using because there was no other word in his deficient dictionary that could even come close to describing his emotions.

He could talk with this girl. He could talk. He could talk. He could talk!

When Anu Met Lizzy

He did not quite put his finger on the right pulse. Why did that day seem to be the best day in his life? Was it because of the fact that he was in America? Was it because of the sights and sounds of New York? Or was it because of the fact that he was in love with the prettiest girl he had ever met?

The whole day had been a melodious song. Right from the Statue of Liberty, to the Met- the Metropolitan museum, the Village, everything had been magical. But at the end of it, he was inclined to agree that had he even been in Nagpur with her that day, it would still have been the best day of his life. This is what love does to your life! It makes you complete.

It was almost eleven at night now. And while they had been running around hot dog vendors and the like, yet it was time to eat something. All the walking and running around — *yes, these crazy Americans walk, even though they have the best of everything around them* — had just gone on to make them both equally famished.

"You know what?" she began. "I just love all kinds of Indian food. But since it's your first day here in America, and we have already eaten enough burgers and hot dogs, our cuisine is basically done with, why don't we go and have a pizza or something?"

That sounded interesting. Once he agreed, she immediately dragged him into a small little diner across the corner on 51st Street which apparently made the best pizzas in the whole of America. *Kinda hot claim to make considering the size of America… Hey, whaddayaknow? I am speaking American already!*

As soon as they walked in, Anurag was stunned to see the place teeming with people everywhere, jukeboxes playing, large groups all around and business in full swing. In Delhi, by 11, even Connaught Place starts to die down, irrespective of whatever people say or believe.

"You know what?" he began as soon as they found a little space that had been left for them by the masses of New York. "This place reminds me a lot of Pop's…"

She was still making herself comfortable when she heard his idea. The first response was the natural one. "Who?"

"You know… Pop Tate!" *Come on, light a bulb in there.*

"Ah! The gang? Goodness, you know more about America than I do…" she smiled across to him.

"Nah! It's just that Archie and the Gang gave me my first idea about America. Seriously, but, there is no town called Riverdale, right?"

"Hehehehe! No, there is none… but Rochester will surely seem like Riverdale to you. It has these quaint little places, quiet little eateries. It really is much better than New York. This place is a fish market. What'll you have?"

One nano second earlier and he would have made the blunder of a lifetime. What was actually about to slip through his newly-found courageous mouth was "You". And that would have been the end of it all. And you don't really have to be intelligent to figure out why. But he stopped himself. Somehow. He did not know how.

But even before he could get to answer her question, she had something more to say to him, "Where are you staying for the night?"

Dehydrated. Completely. His face lost all blood. Why was she asking this? Did she want to stay with him? Was she going to spend the night with him in case he was staying some place? *America rocks!*

But back to the issue at hand. America may rock, but he didn't. His original plans had no place for sleeping. It was New York for the night. He knew that the city did not sleep, so why would he? Particularly since he was going to be there for just one night.

Her question needed an answer still but he was nowhere near giving one. Where was she staying originally? That was also a pertinent question, only that he could not be the one to go ahead and ask it. The best answer, he decided, was to tell her what the scene really was.

"I'm not staying anywhere. In the sense that I just wanted to roam all around New York tonight. I had an option between a Bed and Breakfast and a locker near Grand Central and I took the latter." *It's her move now. What the hell am I talking about? "Move"? What does that even mean!! What has gotten into me? Am I thinking of having sex with her now? No wait, not 'having sex', but am I thinking of scoring tonight? Yes, you moron, that's the thing to focus on right now.*

And when the answer came, it took him so much by surprise that he felt like going into one of the ovens in the kitchen and baking himself once and for all. "Good. My folks live here, just a little outside the Village and they're visiting my grandma in Florida now. So we could go and stay there for the night. And then leave together in the morning and catch the 8:21 to Buffalo. Whaddyasay?"

Oh bloody hell!

"S...s...s...u...r...r...e!"

Didn't make much sense, but at least it got the job done!

"So, good. Now here's the plan. We are in no rush to go anywhere. Why don't we finish eating and then head out for Max's?"

"Who is he? Friend of yours?" *Natural response.*

"Oh no," she began with a small little laugh that once again sent those ripples down his spine. *Damn it!* "Max's is a pub down 41st. It plays great music and, after eleven, the booze is like real cheap. You are 21, right?"

"Uh, yes… I am 21. But… Tonight…" Now this was the fag end of it. Everything was going overboard today. First he had said that he had trouble speaking to girls, but then he somehow, through no fault of his own though, had managed to get invited to stay the night at her place where they'd be alone, and now he was going to have to tell her that he wasn't quite a drinker. How much could she take? And she was the one. The real one.

"What's tonight? You don't have anything to do, right?" and she laughed. That was it. The decision was being made. He had to risk it.

"No, like if we get too drunk we might miss the train tomorrow morning. So…" *Nice try.*

"Oh don't worry… we'll be up in time. It'll be fun. New friends, partying all night. Hey, hello America!" and she spread out her hands and turned it all around, her face beaming with a smile that showed her perfectly crafted teeth. Oh, he had never seen a girl so pretty! He had never had this experience before in his life. No girl had ever done this to him.

"If you say so… then fine. We can go!"

The pizza arrived. She literally tore through it, forcing him to swallow his food and chew at the same time. They had to get to Mark's or wherever. Apparently, it couldn't wait!

Even as he tried to push for the bill, she snatched it away from him and figured it out herself. Her reasoning was simple, "Your first day in my country. I'm not letting you pay for anything!" And soon they were out of there once again, running down the street. It seemed she was intoxicated and they hadn't even started drinking as yet.

Max's was one wonderful place, something quite like, well, nothing he had seen in India. And when he saw the prices of alcohol there, even by conversion they appeared much cheaper than the costs at home. Which was weird! Unbelievable is more like it. No wonder people loved to stay in America. It was the place to be in. It was the place where life was cheap and yet more convenient. All the dreams that he had seen about the country were true. Real true.

"What'll you have?" she asked.

And Anurag kept staring at her. He didn't know one drink from the other and here she was asking him for his opinion. All he had drank till date was scotch, the after effects of which were not pleasant. All that he knew was that he would not have that drink ever again. Never. Not today, at least. So after twisting his lips this side and that side and shaking his head from left to right, basically acting his pants off, he said, "Scotch makes me very drowsy. Anything else will do!"

"Scotch? Who do you think I am, the Queen of England? How about some shots?" And she made her eyes go round and round again, something that made him want to just get up and hold her face in his hands and look into those eyes forever.

"Sure… sounds good to me!" *Shots? Shots! Sounds good. Must be some diluted crap which girls drink. That should be safe for me.*

And she pulled herself up on a bar stool, turned to what looked like Max himself and asked him to 'fill it up'. Max only smiled in reply, shaking his head as if he remembered some great joke and placed two small glasses in front of them.

Anurag looked around the place for sometime – people were evidently having fun there, some were flirting, some were acting weird and some were just sitting blankly. When he turned back towards the stand, he saw that his 'shot' was lying in front of him, while Lizzy spoke to Max about something. *Do they know each other?* And this was a shot? A shot? Really? It seriously was a shot, a shot of nothing. Goodness! Who wastes money drinking these small pegs of vodka, or whatever it is? Why drink it? These mustn't be good worth anything!

And then she finished her little conversation with the bartender and said, "Bottom's up!" Thankfully he knew what that meant. Seeing her pick her little bar measure up, he too followed suit and in synchronized movement they both placed their pegs on their lips and tilted their heads all the way back.

When he awoke next morning, he found himself in his shorts, sleeping on a bed, with Lizzy sleeping right next to him. It was three in the afternoon.

The Games
People Play

"I don't know what happened! I was right there with you. We did come back home, or else why would we be lying here on my bed? Stop freaking out will you? It's no big deal!"

Lizzy kept jumping here and there around the bed, her blanket held around her by both hands. She just kept tossing and turning, looking for something. Anurag just kept staring at the ceiling, dumbstruck. He just remembered the first shot that he had taken with her. Everything after that was all blank. However hard he tried, nothing seemed to come back. Nothing.

"I know everyone there at college. Don't worry, I'll help you get settled there. We'll take another train. School's closed as it is right now. So stop worrying so much!" And she pushed him aside to see if what she was searching for was under him by any chance.

Anurag was feeling both irritated and rather scared. He had not seen her properly since the moment he had woken up, since he was wondering all the time about how to get to the University, how to get started with the process, how to book new train tickets and the like. And here she was, turning round and round and round, pushing and pulling him. The excitement of last night had died down and though he was shit scared, he was also getting irritated with the way she was behaving now -- showing no signs of any concern for the situation.

He turned his head towards her, and screamed, "What the hell are you doing? Do you realize what kind of a fuck up we are in now?"

"Shut up, will you? I can't find my bra!" And she continued her search!

Anurag got up so fast that he almost fell out of the bed. "Your bra? Bra? Why don't you have your bra on you? Are you not wearing anything under those blankets?" *Crisis! Now what?*

"No, I don't! Why else do you think I'm holding this up on me?" As it is she was unable to find what she was looking for, and here he was asking stupid questions. It wasn't quite unnatural for her to flare up instantly.

But Anurag had other concerns. He wasn't bothered about whether she slept with her bra on or not, whether she slept with anything on or not, all he was bothered about at that moment was whether something had happened between them last night. He just kept staring at her, his eyes about to pop out of their sockets any moment and his mouth agape, big enough to let a dinosaur in. One of the large ones at that!

And what got him even more twisted inside was why she wasn't bothered about it. The question there was not where her bra was, but whether it was him that had taken the bra off the previous night. And then again, how could he? He wasn't the one who could take off bras? He didn't even know what a bra looked like properly, just because he had been too ashamed to go to porn sites himself in the first place.

And then it was not only all about the bra. When bras came off, something else supposedly went on. And he sure as hell never remembered buying anything. How could he when he remembered nothing of the night before after the first shot. What was in that small drop of a glass? Had Max spiked his drink? Was that what she was telling him? Was this whole thing a set up to rob him of something?

But then he had to throw out that thought right away because he could still feel her jumping all around him, upturning blankets, bed sheets and pillows, searching for that truant bra. If they did have sex, he couldn't remember anything of it, because he was too drunk. And that made him want to cry. Badly. This was not how he had hoped his virginity would be spent.

But then again, perhaps they hadn't done it! That was still on the cards. After all, why would either of them want to go the whole way without a condom? Not possible!

Americans were wise in such matters. She wouldn't want an unknown guy who had just moved from India going inside her without adequate protection. It just didn't add up.

"It's not here... damn! Where has it gone?" She plopped herself right in the middle of the bed, trying to widen her search to the other areas in the room. As he lay next to her, he saw her properly then for the first time that morning. Or was it afternoon? In the light of day, she was still the prettiest thing he had ever seen in his whole life. Her unkempt sizzling blonde hair fell all around her face and her delicate fingers clasped the blanket around her breasts. He wanted to see them once again since he couldn't remember. He wanted to touch them. He wanted to...

"Do you think I took it off somewhere else?" She was biting her lip and driving him berserk now. Just the look of her in that state. He needed to let go. Something, somewhere. And since she was driving him crazy all over again, and since *it* didn't feel any different from last night, perhaps nothing really had happened. Not to mention the surefire clinch — the case of the missing condom(s). He needed to take a leak. Do something. Not just stare at her.

He got off the bed, moving through all the mess that had been created by the blankets and sheets, and walked away from there. His legs felt weird, but that must be because of all the drinking they had done the previous night. He needed to take a leak. But he had no idea where the bathroom was. He started walking around the room, trying to look for a door.

He had never ever been to a house like this before. He had seen them in movies though—Hollywood films. It was like one of those standard American homes you see in Hollywood movies. It had sunlight coming in from everywhere and everything inside looked spick-and-span.

As he begun to walk around, he saw several doors around him. He opened one and found a closet with clothes flowing out of it. *These Americans are crazy! A small room to hang clothes in?* The second door was luckily the bathroom. Again, such clean and crystal loos were only found in posh hotels in India. That too the ones in the metros.

The marble throne was shining on the opposite wall. Anurag walked towards it and picked up the lid. He kept looking around even as he got into the position to let go. Before letting go, he looked down once to make sure that he'd get the aim right and then he just stopped. Even as he held the little general down there, waiting to explode, it just got sucked right back in. And it wasn't that he even wanted to give it a try. It just wasn't going to go. It was finally solved.

He tried to look away, thinking perhaps that that would make the whole incident disappear. His eyes fell to the back of the door, the reflection of which was now being brazenly telecasted on the bathroom mirror and he saw something else. It was proven now. No mistake about it. Q.E.D!

He picked up the thing hanging behind the bathroom door and walked out again, back to where she was on the bed. He threw it right at her and sat down on the small little stool beside the bed, dumbstruck. He did not know which way to turn.

Or what to do.

"Where on earth did you get this?" she asked, picking it up.

No reply.

"Come on… I've been searching it for so long and you just picked it up out of nowhere. Where was it? Tell me…" she persisted.

No reply.

"Oh come on now… Don't worry. I told you I'll take care of everything. We'll move to Rochester in a while and I'll fix you up with everything over there. You'll just have nothing to worry about. Trust me!"

No reply.

"Fine… have it your way!"

And she somehow managed to magically slip on her bra while still behind the blankets and also put on her top. She then squeezed herself out of bed and went to the loo. She was back soon enough. Very soon enough.

She crawled towards him. One step at a time. Looking at him. Softly. Gently. Shocked. She could not keep looking at him. Surely she was having trouble in identifying her emotions. She just walked gingerly and sat at the foot of the bed. Her toes kept scratching at the rug below, making tiny circles or squares or some basic geometric shape that he didn't bother identifying. It was all gloom. The bathroom was killing people today.

There was a long pause. A long, long pause. It wasn't exactly a pause, it was a whole muted minute which seemed to run longer than a decade. It was as if time had washed itself away from all the clocks on the earth and was just waiting for them to make the first move. Anyone. Anyhow. She knew he wasn't going to say anything. His head was still in his hands, making circles with his fist around his eyes.

"Did we…?"

He looked up finally. He wasn't crying or anything, but he looked tense, sad, lost. It was like he was taken advantage of, by her. This was weirder than just his face. His look told her that he didn't know what to say.

"Maybe we didn't… maybe it was just you!" Perhaps there was another solution to the riddle.

But he was now ready to talk. And not just mumble. T-A-L-K.

"Me? Alone? In a condom? How sick do you think I am?" he burst out. It was bad enough that they had slept together last night, for no apparent reason other than being bone drunk, and now she was making silly suggestions to make it seem all the more trivial.

"Oh… Well don't worry! What happened, happened. Nothing we can do about it now!" She was being practical about it. But who wanted practical? Ever?

"How can you say that? We just made love last night…"

"Woah! Hold it there… Made love? What rubbish are you talking about. We just had sex. Plain and simple! We were drunk and we made a mistake! What's with all this 'made love' business? Calm down!" Now it was her turn to seem irritated. Fine, so they had done it. It wasn't a big deal and here he was, taking it to some altogether different level. Matter of fact, it was no level, it was beyond all levels. This was chaos.

But this got him all the more flabbergasted. "What the hell are you saying? Did it not mean anything to you?"

"Mean? Neither of us have any recollection of it. And what the fuck do you mean about it meaning anything. You aren't Aaron. With him it means something, with you it was just like that… happened!"

Aaron?

The Other Side of
the Tunnel

Finally, the train pulled out of Grand Central. The rough ride of New York was now over. And he was on a train to Rochester, but he had no idea where he was headed. Lizzy was seated next to him, but the spark between them had now grown cold. It had become a mess. While she seemed to be at peace with this mess, he was going bananas inside.

The image of her flaring up sitting on the foot of the bed was still knocking all around inside his head. He had no recollection of the act the first time he had ever done it and, to make matters worse, the girl he had done it with wanted to put it behind her instantly and move on. She wanted to label it as a mistake. Nothing more, nothing less. This was so not the way he had wanted it to happen with him the first time. Anything but this!

And she was not just another girl, she was the girl that he had thought was his first love. This was the girl with whom he had spent a whole day after knowing her for something like five minutes. She was the girl who had not made him stammer, and that by itself was a huge achievement. She had made him feel like a different person, something altogether different from who he really was. She was the girl who had slept with him for the first time. These things didn't happen with him, these things *never* happened with him.

Though there were many pros in this case, one con stood out and it changed the whole equation altogether.

And there was someone *else*. Not only did the good stuff never happen to him, even the bad stuff stayed away from him. All the way through. But no, that was not it. This was not the way it should have gone.

But though it was weird — not weird actually, sad would be the more apt word — it was true that all this made him feel like his old usual self. It reaffirmed his faith in his theory that everything in the world was out to screw him. Since now he was in America, it was perhaps happening at a much brisker rate than the usual laidback speed with which it used to happen back home.

Here he was, sitting in a train going from New York to Rochester to study at the University there – his childhood dream and revenge motif – sitting next to the girl he was in love with, and with whom he had just had sex, but yet everything seemed to be falling apart. Still.

And he could not understand her one bit. Here she was apparently in a relationship with this Aaron guy or whoever, and she was fine about having slept with some other guy, one who was more or less a stranger to her. Was he too allowed to do the same thing? Meaning, could he go around sleeping with others? Then what made relationships special? Is this the 'open relationship' you read about in Facebook and other similar places? What sense did it make? For whom?

But this wasn't the time for higher philosophies. It was a time to introspect and to try and apprehend the route further. It seemed like she was not going to talk to him anymore, for clearly she was pissed at him for trying to make their love-making more special that she liked to believe it was. So again he would be in Rochester, friendless once again. And then he considered the prospect that if all American girls had similar outlook on relationships, they were all dead to him.

He was lost. Literally.

He was completely lost in thought, when he heard something from beside him. By the time he could come back to reality, he saw Lizzy looking at him, and it seemed that she wanted an answer from him for a question she had asked but he had not heard.

"Sorry, what..?"

"Just do me a favor. Don't tell anyone about anything that happened between us… Let it just be between you and me!" she said.

As if I was going to telecast to the world that the first time I had sex with a girl – that too one I was in love with – is seeing someone else and wants to forget it as a mistake.

"Sure... I understand..." and he turned away from her.

But then she placed her hand on his shoulder. It was similar to passing 550 volts of raw electric current through him. Why do this now? He had got her opinion on the matter and he knew it had been nothing, could never be anything. Why do this now?

"Why are you getting so upset? I really like you a lot... I have never had so much fun with anyone before. I really don't want to lose you over such a stupid thing!" she continued. This was killing him. It was like someone had stabbed a fork in his eyes and was now twisting it around, prying it lose from its sockets.

It was too much. She needed to know. Or did she? He tossed the idea in his mind for a while and decided that it would be much better to tell her how he felt, what he felt inside him about her and about whatever had happened between them. She needed to know. *She cannot just brush it aside. Not like this.*

He kept looking at her all this while, forlorn, love torn. It was a miracle that she wasn't able to comprehend anything just by looking at his face which was full of strange and animated expressions. He needed courage to speak to her about this. He wasn't used to all this. But he kept reminding himself that he'd have to do it. *Like tearing off a bandage in one smooth motion — fast and effective.*

"Lizzy, you need to know something. This doesn't happen to me!" he began, thinking this was the best way to start.

"What doesn't happen to you?" Her face gave it all away. She was clueless.

"Remember I told you about me and girls? How I can't talk to any of them? Just like I had talked to you earlier, when we had just met… and you had asked me whether there was a problem somewhere with me…you remember that, right?" *Is she listening to me?*

"Yes, I do… go on…" *Apparently she is.*

"So everything that happened between you and me… it was special for me! I…"

"Oh I know… It was good for me too. But let's keep it at that. Why spoil what was good for me for a small mistake?" She had *other* ideas!

"No, you don't understand. You were the first girl to do something like that to me. It was experiencing something that I had never felt till I met you…"

"Oh fuck! No! Seriously?"

That sounded a little positive. And he jumped at it. If he said it right then and there, perhaps there was still a chance for him. For *them.*

"Yes Lizzy! Yes… I fell in love with you right from the moment I saw you!"

"Oh fuck me hard Lord! Fucking shit… what? I was like the first girl you could talk to by quirk of fate, and you arrived at the conclusion that it was love and all that shit? That's not love… it's just a feeling you had!"

"I know what I felt… Don't tell me about what I felt. It's just that you did not feel the same." He was protesting now, seeing his words being dismissed as if they meant nothing.

"Come on now out of it... you just spent one fuckin' day with me. How could you fall in love with me in that time! Where on earth are you getting all this from? Seriously!"

"I am telling you, I know it is love because it is unlike any other thing that I have ever felt. You might not believe it, but I do..."

"Listen to me, you dork! Whatever you are thinking, you're thinking wrong! Alright? There is no love-dove, never was. Love is what I and Aaron have, alright! You'll know when you see it tomorrow. He too studies at the univ. Meet him, then you'd know! Till then, just stop it!" And she turned away from him, looking straight ahead at the seat in front. A sign of protest perhaps.

"Love is what I and Aaron have, alright!"

Eh?

The Other Guy

Rochester was nothing like what he had imagined America to be, as in not the America that he was acquainted with through Hollywood. This was more like a *F.R.I.E.N.D.S.* kind of set up and he knew from just the look of it that he had just stepped into real America. Not that the business section of the city did not have those huge tall, glass paneled buildings that is trademarked America. But it was the quainter residential sections of the place that caught his attention. Oh it was huge. It was all America, it was real good America. What happened to him on seeing Rochester for the first time was surely love. And this love would remain, and be reciprocated. He was sure of that.

The main university building was like an old colonial castle. Moat and all included. As in it wasn't all that of a moat as it was an island where the main University campus was located. They had to drive through a long bridge to reach it from Rochester. And all that Anurag could notice were the wooden houses that were littered in an organized manner throughout. Wooden. *Wooden.* This was new. Why would anyone live in houses made of wood? What happened when it rained? What kind of a house did parents leave for their children here in America? A house full of termites? Anurag tried to do the math, but it could not add up. Sure, he had seen these houses a lot in American movies and sitcoms, but to actually see them *in the wood* was quite a different experience for Anurag.

He couldn't believe he would be studying and living here for the next two years. He could almost taste his experience there. It was nothing like anything he had felt all his life. As a matter of fact, he was so enamored by all the sights and sounds around him that he was able to take Lizzy and her so called "love of my life" Aaron off his mind .

But let's give the devil her due: Lizzy did help Anurag with the entire admission process and even got all his papers sorted out. Apparently she had been at Rochester for a long, long time, studying different things. She never wanted to leave and join the outside world. She had planned her whole life behind the university walls with that smug bastard Aaron. *Damn!*

After the basic formalities were over, his hostel accommodation was fixed in the D Block of the premises, room 212, and he was to share it with a certain Aaron Reznor. Yes, *him.* She fixed it. According to her, it would be better if they all lived together, for what else were friends for? He didn't like it, but on what grounds could he possibly argue!

After they had got him his room, they walked around the university campus for a while, through the abundant greens and the cobbled pathways, both of which were a rarity at home. Everything was clean and in place. There were no posters anywhere of elected student officials, which usually are either torn or jostling for space on university walls back home. Here there was no such thing. There were simply notice boards, which held messages of seminars and workshops, and memos from teachers and students alike, and some even personal advertisements — for instance, Kevin was looking for a customer to buy his iPod.

She led him around a roundabout which was surrounded by old buildings, which seemed much more resilient than the new buildings being built around Gurgaon today. After leaving three buildings on the right, they turned into the fourth one. Block D. His room was on the second floor.

Even the floors and stairs of the hostel were spick and span, clean all the way through. If he could not have found anything better, he could even have lived right there under the stairs! They ran up two flights of stairs and took a turn to the left because the proper signs on the wall at the landing told them to do so. Just like a hotel.

Soon they were in front of Room 212. He had reached there first but then she suddenly came up running, plonked the bags she was carrying and before he could even knock on the door, she sprang from behind him and, breaking through the barricade his bags had made and almost crashing through the door, she ran inside. He decided to stand there and be polite. All he wanted was to not have to see *them* get cozy.

But there was no escaping that. It was just a room with two tables and two beds and two chairs. And one loo, which, though closed at the moment, did not look very promising considering the space in the room even did not look enough. *Surely two people couldn't get in there at once.* Which was perhaps a good thing.

But the problem was that he could see everything, even as he stood outside and tried to avert his gaze. They were right there, tongues going everywhere, searching for stuff inside each other's mouths. She was turned away from him and his face was hidden behind the back of her head. But what he could make out from the overlapping body structure of the mesh before him was that Aaron Reznor was about his height, perhaps an inch or two taller, and had an athletic figure. Even as she pressed herself against him, it seemed that not even a small little square inch of his flesh sunk in back into him. He was tough, surely very tough. Seeing her and seeing him, one thing became certain in Anurag's mind, he came nowhere close to match the two amazingly good looking people. He was surely the odd one out. And perhaps he could have understood that and made himself comfortable with it but… he was a man madly in love. And it was his first love. And now it was looking like his last.

"Aaron, this is my friend… we met yesterday at Grand Central and he is new to our country. Anurag, this is Aaron, the love of my life!" He heard everything, but the last line. Selective deafness it was called, perhaps.

Both men extended their hands, but surprisingly, Aaron's shake was a lot warmer than Anurag's. It seemed like he was truly welcoming Anurag to his country, his city, his university, his dorm room and into his life. He seemed to hold no malice. He seemed to be a warm person, one you could be friends with right from the word go. But then, if you had slept with his girlfriend the night before, you were forced to ask yourself some questions about your analysis.

"Hey there man! Put it up… Aaron Reznor, your new pal and roommate! Lizzy did message about you yesterday… I was expecting you both to land up here much earlier. Overslept, did ya?" And while he smiled on completing his speech, Anurag wanted to just stab himself.

"Yes… Just! Late night…"

"Hey dude, I'm no girl… you can talk to me at least, can't you?"

So Lizzy did tell him everything about him. Except the bit about later that night.

"Will take a little time. I can speak a lot more freely with Lizzy now!"

"Then it's just a matter of one night I guess… Come on in… Here, let me help ya!"

The two boys got a little busy in pushing Anurag's luggage inside. Even Lizzy helped, which was quite a wonder, since Delhi girls just order about and not do anything in such situations. They want to be treated like equals, but retain their girly confirmation. American girls on the other are hands on, like men, only much prettier!

After they had settled down, Aaron lit a cigarette, after offering Anurag one, and with Lizzy on his lap, gave Anurag a whole sitting--tour of the University.

"Hey man, since you ate a lot of pizzas and hot dogs yesterday, how about we try some Indian food today?" His voice was deep and foggy, perhaps because of the cigarettes, but it was a charismatic sound, something that made you forget everything else and listen. "So once we are all a bit rested and ready, let's all go down and grab some food at that Taj Mahaal place down the street?"

"Taj Mahal?"

"It's either Taj Mahal, or Bombay, or Delhi here in the States. You don't get a large range. And Lizzy and I are just crazy about Indian food. Spicy, saucy, and it's like a full big meal. Not a snack that you chew when coming out of the gym!" *Oh man, he uses 'coming out of the gym' as a passing phrase!*

"Sure, we can go and eat there… Will make me feel a lot more at home!"

"Cool! They make the best chicken tattis around there, I have heard!"

Anurag had just started sipping his coffee but, on

hearing this, the sip he had taken came shooting out of his mouth, smearing itself over everything that lay in its path.

"What?"

"What happened bro?"

"Anurag? You ok?" Even Lizzy chipped in, her eyes showing genuine concern. Aaron tried to reach out to him, just to make sure that he wasn't going to die or something.

Trying very hard to control his urge to puke, Anurag uttered, "What did you say we'll eat there?"

"Chicken tatt…"

"Oh no no no! Dude, it's chicken tikka you're talking about! Right?"

"Could be dude! But what's the big deal?"

"Because tatti means… uh…you know, doing it… tatti means that!"

"Doing it? You mean sex? In India sex is called doing tatti?"

"Oh God! No no, not doing that… doing the other thing…"

"Gays do tatti?"

"Arre, even you and I and Lizzy do tatti!"

Aaron's jaw dropped. His words took a while before coming through his lips, "You mean a threesome is called doing a tatti?"

"Goodness, it has nothing to do with sex!! Tatti means going to the restroom every morning and sitting there and doing stuff from the backside!"

"Shit?"

"No no, it's the thing you do… We all do!"

"Ya, that's what I am saying… Shitting… is that what tatti means?"

"Yes Shit mean potty? I just thought you were saying 'Shit' like you Americans always say…"

"Ya, I get it… potty! Tatti! Poo… Duty!"

"Duty?"

Lizzy jumped in. "Ok, this can take a while. Anu, I am sure you'll get through with the slangs later on…"

"I know American slangs!" *I am no less that your boyfriend. I know everything. He eats potty at Taj Mahal.*

"Then you should know what duty means!" She was trying to put and end to this.

"You Americans call duty a slang? I thought here work meant worship! The capitalism song!"

"Oh goodness me!" And Aaron starting laughing. Lizzy began to laugh as well. But Anurag couldn't see what was funny. *Are they laughing at the situation or at me? They must be laughing at me! Oh, no!*

Anurag didn't quite know whether he was miffed at what had just happened or amused or, for that matter, disgusted. Aaron was scoring more points with Lizzy than Anurag could even imagine scoring. And here he was, trying to rectify one of Aaron's mistakes, and getting the wrong end of the stick himself.

It has been quite a long journey for him. First India to America and then New York to Rochester. And the whole process, ever since last night, had been grueling on Anurag. And to make matters worse, the first girl that he had ever had sex with was undoubtedly in love with someone else.

It happened. On such occasions, when he felt self-conscious, humiliated, it always happened to him — each and every time. Without exception. He tried to control it, but it was pointless, Anurag had realized this a long time back. In school, whenever he would be in such a morbid state, he would feel the need to go and do it. Shit. His bowels always buckled up. His parents initially feared that it was some kind of intestinal disease, but later, after many visits to the doctor, they realized that their fears were unjustified. It was not an intestinal disease, it was just plain and simple, good old-fashioned fear of being mocked at, just plain panic!

And it had begun to manifesting itself in his stomach again. In front of Lizzy and Aaron. In his dorm room in Rochester, United States of America. And Anurag needed to get a move on things. Run.

Just then, Aaron and Lizzy stopped laughing and Lizzy said, "Ok! Ok! Enough! Anu, I am sure you'll learn all the American slangs staying here … Right now, I am hungry as hell. So can we all go down to eat that Chicken Tatti?"

"Tikka!" Anurag said.

"Whatever!"

"Excuse me, but can I use the restroom once before we leave?" Anurag asked nervously.

"Ok, old chap!" said Aaron.

Anurag had no idea who the "old chap" was amongst them. But he let it pass as just another American expression. Aaron was beaming, ear to ear. He had made a native of the alien. He was good. He picked himself up from his cushioned mattress and grabbed Lizzy too. He knew it better to leave at once rather than start another conversation.

Fifteen minutes later, finally ready, Anurag came out.

"Look, look, look… see who the cat dragged out!" Aaron was smiling, ear to ear. They were sitting on the steps of the hostel, trying to play some game with their fingers.

"What cat?"

"Anu, relax! Just another Yankee talk! Cat dragged out is just trying to say 'Look who's here'… Get it?"

"Seriously, why do you people talk that way? Why talk of a cat when there is no cat?"

"Dude, you want to start on a debate that heads right back to the Declaration of Independence?"

"Why would I want to do that?"

"Dude, I was being disingenuous! Now come on, it's been forever, let's just head to Taj Mahaal. I can eat a whole human being now!"

Aaron placed his ample large hands around Anurag's shoulders and nearly dragged him out of his spot. Anurag felt like a little kid, out for a walk with his elder brother. But the fact of the matter was that Aaron was the same age as Anurag. No more, no less. It just looked that way because of the size.

The three of them kept walking for some time, till they reached some kind of a parking lot. There were not a lot of cars parked there, but Aaron had his car in that lot. Anurag had expected Americans to have those jazzy cars —but he realized it was not the case. Of all the cars parked there, none of them looked anything quite like what Anurag had expected. They were just simple cars, like the standard Chevy Aveo or Maruti Zen category cars. *An average Indian has a better looking car!*

But not better than Aaron Reznor's. The car he owned was not a standard run-of-the-mill contraption. Aaron owned a black custom-painted Camaro, with dark blue vinyl running all through the body of the vehicle. It was one of the coolest cars that Anurag had ever seen. Right out of a Hollywood movie. The insides had leather upholstery, that wrapping right into the contours of Anurag's body. It was a feeling experienced never before.

"Hey man, check this out... I got the car modified!" Aaron was naturally extremely proud of his transportation.

"Modified?" Anurag knew precious little about cars and the way they functioned. All he cared about was the basic look of the car and whether it could take him from one place to another safely or not.

"Ya, like you know... replaced the engine, transmission, suspension... stuff like that. I even thought of getting nitrous fixed, but I guess that would have been too Vin Diesel!"

Anurag was having a lot of trouble putting up with the American English — everyone seemed to be in a habit of leaving out whole actual necessary words from sentences. *That would have been too Vin Diesel? What the hell!* But he had to keep up the pretense of understanding things at one go. Just to keep up with them.

"Nitrous is like a jet, right? It comes out like gas and makes the car go faster?"

"No, no, not like that! Nitrous jet streams the car! But cops go nuts the minute they see a car exhuming the spray and it's not exactly street legal. So no point!"

What on earth is he talking about? And in what language is he speaking it? All of it was floating past Anurag's head. Quite like Nitrous. But he had understood that Aaron had basically changed the factory settings of his car. Personalized it. This car was what he would not have got had he bought a Camaro from a showroom.

When the car started, the engine revved up a sound that almost shattered Anurag's ear drums. It was like a tractor starting. Anurag felt himself sinking further into the leather seats. His hands were desperately trying to grab hold of something. Anything. To hold on to, in case the car left him behind, along with something called nitrous! The engine rev continued as Aaron drove the car out of the university complex and hit the main road.

For the first few minutes, Anurag had a very low opinion of Aaron as a driver. For starters, he was driving at the wrong end of the road. But, then, realizing that everyone was making the same mistake, Anurag recalled that the US roads worked the other way round. He was not able to take in much of the surroundings for the dastardly noise from below the hood of the car kept him on tenterhooks all the while. From what little he could make of the city, Rochester seemed like the finest place he had seen. It was modern and modest — just the best combination someone could have asked for. The hustle and bustle of NYC was missing, and yet the enigma that is America was lavishly printed all over the place.

It was very difficult to get even one word across to the people in the front seat and it was not only because of the sound-polluting engine. Aaron was a heavy metal fan, and some weird sounding man was screaming for no rhyme or reason through the car audio speakers. Not one word was clear, nor was the intention. And every red light at which the car stopped, Aaron bobbed his head left and right, forwards and backwards. He labeled it as "head banging", but Anurag could not grasp what he was banging his head against. Lizzy later cleared it for him, explaining that head banging in metal was a signature move. It still made no sense to Anurag.

Finally, after many lefts and rights, they arrived at Taj Mahal, which had the words *Food Parlor* written underneath its name. Anurag didn't quite know what to make of it. But Aaron and Lizzy seemed to be excited to the hilt. As they walked in, Anurag realized that Taj Mahal was basically a kind of McDonald's serving Indian food. *Perhaps, it is the same with all eateries in America. Maybe everything here looks like McDonald's.*

The attendant behind the counter looked like an Indian, or a Pakistani, or a Sri Lankan (basically from the *Region*). From the looks of it, he seemed to be a student. For all that mattered, he could have even been in Anurag's class. It was one of the most popular ways in which overseas students in the States made some cash for themselves. Aaron led the team inside and marched straight to the counter.

"How can I help you?"

"In many ways…wait," said Aaron. Then he turned towards Lizzy and Anurag and said, "Why don't you go and occupy a table, I will order in the meanwhile."

Aaron begun ordering and Anurag noticed the way in which he spoke to the attendant behind the counter. There was a lot of mutual respect. It wasn't a situation where they were the customers and the man-behind-the-desk their hired slave. They were all equals at that crossing. No one was smaller or bigger than the other. It was something that he had seldom seen back at home.

Aaron completed the ordering and found Lizzy and Anurag sitting behind one of the booths in the premises. Five minutes later, food came rushing in. All of it. It took two guys to carry it to them. And it looked delicious. Anurag's manners drifted away as he tore right into a piece of reshmi kebab along with an apology of a naan. Aaron and Lizzy dug in too.

For the next few minutes not a word was spoken.

Only the faint sound of clattering teeth was heard. Three sets of teeth. After ten minutes, each member of the trio stopped, now satiated. Anurag wanted to burp, but decided to suppress it somehow. Aaron was busy digging his teeth and Lizzy looked ready to die. Aaron mumbled some words out.

"The food here is simply amazing. This is one of my and Lizzy's favorite hangouts!"

"Yes, I agree. This chicken was so amazing… seriously!"

"Dude, there was no chicken in it!"

"It wasn't chicken? No wonder it felt like mutton!"

"Mutton?"

"Goat meat… that's what it was, right?"

"Goat meat? In this?"

"Oh no! What was it then? What on earth did I just eat?"

"Beef! It had beef."

Anurag felt the burp coming back from within. Only that this time it wasn't only a burp. There was something more attached to it. He felt his blood dilating. His stomach was churning. It was a very awkward feeling. Sure, he had puked before. It had happened to him many times when he was sick, or when he overate, or went for swimming classes right after eating breakfast. But this time, it felt slightly different. It felt sick. It felt like someone was hammering away at his insides. Beef. *Beef.* It just kept playing inside his head till it took over all his mental faculties.

"There was beef? I had beef?"

"Dude, you ok?"

Anurag couldn't stop it anymore. He felt the nausea creeping into his throat. He covered his mouth hastily and asked the question with his eyes instead. *Bathroom?* Aaron was a little confused. Lizzy didn't even know where to begin guessing. But the Asian guy behind the counter who had been observing the trio with considerable wonder seemed to understand immediately.

He rushed to the booth and pointed, "This way bro!"

While Lizzy and Aaron kept looking in surprise, the attendant guided Anurag to the restroom and positioned himself outside the door. Just in case. Lizzy and Aaron got up and asked the attendant, "Hey man, what happened? What was that all about?"

"They don't eat beef in India! I guess he didn't realize that… this happens to many Indians when they eat out in America. No biggie!"

"So you're not from India?"

"Hell no! I'm from Pakistan… we eat beef, but it's a religious thing for them. The cow has something to do with Hindu mythology. I think there was a law or something in India, or maybe a joke, that you can get three months for killing a man, but a lifetime sentence for killing a cow. Cow slaughter is a serious issue back in their country!"

"What the…! I had seriously no idea… that's weird!"

"Not really… you wouldn't feed a Jew or a Muslim pork now, would you?"

Anurag emerged from of the washroom a minute later. He looked like a dead man walking. His face was flushed, and, for some reason, he was looking thin too.

"Man, you alright?"

Anurag couldn't speak. The niggling fear at the back of his head was that the minute he'd open his mouth, more stuff would come pouring out. And he didn't want that. He had puked enough already.

Anurag nodded. How could he be alright? He had just had beef! He had gone against the code his parents had brought him up with. Albeit without knowing. But a crime is a crime. And a serious, heinous crime had been committed by him. *The law is clear enough – life imprisonment for cow slaughter! Or was that an SMS joke?*

The attendant was standing next to him and was stroking his back to make him feel better. Aaron and Lizzy had understood the whole matter and had expressions of concern and apology on their faces.

"Here, have some water…" said the attendant. He deserved a vote of thanks surely.

"Thank you! Seriously, I honestly had not known."

"*Hota hain, hota hain! Sabke saath hota hain!* You are not the first Indian I have seen throwing up like that. You see many Indians come to Rochester to study and come here to eat Indian food. And bang, the same thing happens to them for the first time! Normally I would have warned you, but I saw you with them. So I thought you were cool with this stuff!"

Aaron smiled sheepishly. If only the poor chap knew what all had been happening with him since morning!

"Don't worry dude! If you do stuff without knowing, that's not counted against you! You'll be fine…" the attendant continued.

"I know… But still! I had never thought that on my very second day in America, something like this would happen. I guess I let my guard down."

"Don't worry man! See, now you know. Whenever we eat out next, or eat anything for that matter, I'll make sure that we get you chicken stuff. Or vegetarian food. Not till you are ok with eating beef… alright?" said Aaron.

"I'll never be ok with eating beef! Never, ever!"

"Hey, no issues! I got your back!"

Again, Anurag couldn't quite follow how Aaron had his back when it was the attendant who was rubbing it. But it was the second time that day that Aaron had looked after him. He was a nice man, a kind soul. Aaron was a friend. A true friend.

Checkmate

The course lectures were more or less the same as they had been in India. But the classrooms where the lectures happened were different. Way different.

To begin with, they were not classrooms at all. They were more like huge seminar rooms, only that they weren't seminar rooms but classrooms, with neatly painted walls, huge boards and a dais for the lecturer to stand on. There were no benches, but individual chairs which were well cushioned, not the board (or bored) ones that are found in Indian hallows (or gallows) of education.

The professors treated the students as equals and were always ready to learn something from them, and that made the students connect with the teachers very well. There was no "sir" or "madam" going around, rather the professors were always addressed with just their first name, Mr. Hardy or Ms Drew. It was cool, very cool. And Anurag was loving every little bit of it.

Anurag's major was in Economics. But he had to take up some other subjects in his course too, something which had absolutely nothing in common with market shares and GDPs.

"What is the deal with this? Why should I have to take up musicology or astrology? How does it make sense?"

Aaron had the answer ready with him. It almost seemed like he had been expecting it for a long time. "Do you only want to know stuff related to Economics, or do you want to know about other stuff too?"

"Like general knowledge?"

"Well, yeah! You can think of it like that…"

"But why should my major depend on that?"

"Believe me dude! If you aren't marked, you wouldn't study. Doing other subjects is a good way to get in tune with more stuff. Why would you want to limit yourself?"

"Seriously? This makes sense and no sense, all at the same time. So what should I take up here? I am confused as it is…"

Lizzy was quick to jump in. "Musicology. By all means. Coz then we'll be together in class. It's going to be fun — a lot of fun! Believe me!" She was so happy just at the idea of both of them going to classes together that she was almost getting ready to jump and click her feet.

"I know nothing about music!"

"Don't worry man, we'll teach you!" *Aaron surely has a weird sense of humor.*

"Yeah? Teach me what? Metallica or Seventh Degree? You think they'll teach me that in class?"

"I don't know of a band called Seventh Degree!"

"Yeah you don't... because there ain't one! It's just like seventh degree torture when you keep playing that sound you call music in here... I made that one up!"

The joke was well received, and Anurag was one step up with the education system in America.

The classes were fine, everything to do with the university was fine, even Aaron was fine — spending time with him every evening was just great. He was very friendly, conversed with Anurag on every topic under the sun and asked a lot of questions about India — the only problem was that Lizzy came over to their room every evening. And though the very sight of her brought Anurag down to his heavily knocking knees, she immediately saddled herself next to Aaron, his knees bore enough strength to take a gun and knock them both over.

A month later, Aaron came running to him in the library, a place where everyone knew him although he never sat there for more than five minutes — *Go figure, this guy's popular!*

"Hey dude, listen... Can you like stay over at Ronnie's tonight?" Ronnie was this other guy of the group. He was on the rowing squad and was built in the shape of one of those WWF wrestlers and it was all even real. But he was a complete sissy on the inside. All in all, he was a good guy and a friend who was ever ready to help you. Just like Aaron.

"Ya sure, I don't mind... Ronnie knows?"

"Yup! Told him already... Just for one night now..."

"No hassles, bro! What's happening with you tonight?" A very, very natural question.

"Nah! Just Lizzy and me... Spending the night together... You know..." and he gave him a small little punch on his arm, a typical 'put 'em up' sign popular amongst guys. But that small little punch almost displaced Anurag's arm from his shoulder—metaphorically speaking of course. He had dreaded this night for almost forever. But now it was here. And while he had prepared himself for this possibility, he did not know how to respond to Aaron then. He had to fight with himself to get back with a suitable response.

"Ya, I know... you can't imagine!" *Look at my guts! This chap can paste me to the wall and look at me go!*

"Huh?"

"Nothing... Just know what you mean!"

Aaron was a little confused now. He was never confused. Even Anurag was seeing the expression of confusion on his face for the first time. Anurag's words seemed to have taken the wind out of him for a while at least. Aaron could not make out what to make of what Anurag had said. *Anurag and his girlfriend had spent a night together?* He had not thought about anything like this so far, but the way Anurag had said that last sentence was making him suspicious. But he could not quiz Anurag about it in detail. He would have to ask Lizzy and every moment from then on till the time he actually meets her would kill him, that much even Anurag knew.

But what Anurag also knew was that he had punctured Aaron's euphoria. And he felt terrible about it. Right there, at that very minute, while Aaron was talking to him about his night plans, Anurag had made one thing very clear to himself — he would fight for her. He would have to fight for her. Ever since that one night, he had just not been able to get over her. Every single time that he had seen her since—flying into Aaron's arms, giggling away, sitting with him, every single moment—he had just felt like putting his finger through her boyfriend's eyes. *Not anymore.*

"Uh, alright then… I'll see you in a while…" Anurag gathered his books and left, leaving Aaron looking so hard at the table that if he had added a little more concentration to his gaze, the table would have perhaps begun moving. It was the first time that Anurag had had a sort of open confrontation with someone in America. And to think of it, it was the first, self-initiated open confrontation of his life.

But as he walked away, Anurag spent a moment wondering about how things had changed so suddenly. Not only was he this guy's roommate, they were also good friends. And to push the edge in his favor, this guy was someone who went to the gym for *pleasure*. If fists were used, there'd be no way in which Anurag would be able survive. Not to mention that in the event of a fight, Aaron was likely to be backed by his friends. But then, Lizzy was too precious for him to give up. In all these months, seeing her so frequently, talking to her, or just simply standing right next to her – it had all made him feel like a different person altogether. And this kind of a feeling was new for him. He liked it. And right then he realized that he was so much in awe of the new self that he had found within himself, so much in love with the idea of finally being able to be with a girl, and that too one he was in love with, that nothing else mattered.

But his joy at his newly-found bravado lasted only a little while longer. Because no sooner had he set foot in his room that Lizzy came tearing through the door. This time, she was looking for him and not for Aaron. But not in a very good way.

"What did you tell him?"

"What did I tell whom?" *Just look at my gall!*

"Aaron… What did you tell him just now?"

"Nothing!" Anurag was trying his level best to take out his most innocent face from its case, a face that was once his normal face. "He told me to spend the night at Ronnie's and I said fine… Nothing more! What happened?"

"Oh don't act so coy with me… it's not going to work! You think you're pretty smart now, don't you?" She was livid. She was more than livid. She looked mad enough to kill.

"Lizzy, I said nothing. You can do anything to me, but I still stand by what I said. I did not say anything, more so because there was nothing to say. He told me something, he asked me a question, and I agreed. End of story!"

"Listen here Anu, right now, all thanks to you, my boyfriend is out there wondering whether at all we slept together that night in New York. He has been so pleasant about it till now, but because of your smart lip, we are going through a relationship crisis! Do you know how much that bloody hurts?"

"Lizzy, listen… I know that night meant nothing to you! But it meant the whole world to me. Imagine what goes through me each and every time I see you in his arms. You don't think there was even an iota of love between the two of us, but for me, it was completely different…"

He stopped to grab his breath. This was the first time that he had ever gone on such a huge monologue to prove his point. Forget proving, this was the first time in his whole life that he was actually making his point. A personal point. Lizzy was staring down at him, her look was now confused. His last line was bound to have had some impact. You cannot mistreat the person who declares his love for you, whatever be the issue at hand.

But Lizzy was going through a different set of ideas in her head. Naturally, all that Anurag was telling her was something that she already knew, but yet it seemed kind of fresh to her at that moment. And even though she tried to assimilate and understand what Anurag was getting to, her mind could not help wonder about Aaron and the hazardous state he was in. He was furious. Had to be. His girlfriend had had sex with a guy only after sixteen hours of meeting him. How could she? And she couldn't help but ask herself — *how could I?*

But what was done was done. And even though it had happened, it had only been a mere hiccup. Otherwise there was just Aaron in her life before that, and had been Aaron in her life since then. The problem though, was that the hiccup did not want to forget everything. He wanted to stay on. And now that was threatening her relationship with Aaron. And somehow, something told her that she just could not allow it to be threatened like that.

She had to interrupt. Break him off at mid-expose.

"Listen, I know it meant something to you. But try and understand, there was nothing in it for me. It was maybe just lust and we were drunk. Very drunk. We did not even know each other well enough to even have any inkling of love. Aaron is the one I love. And I will continue to love him. And there is nothing you can do about it."

Beaten. There was nothing he could do beyond this. She did not love him. Not one bit. She wouldn't love him even if Aaron were to go away. *But would he? It is worth a shot.*

"And I am doing nothing about it. If he loves you as much as I do, he'll love you even when he knows what happened between us. Not that I'll tell him anything. Whatever happened back there in the library was just a slip of the tongue. It just brought back some memories. But I didn't tell him anything that might even remotely suggest that you and I did it that night. If he is drawing his own conclusions, it means he knows something and now he is putting it to test."

Now this got her thinking.

"What do you mean?"

"All I'm saying is that I said something completely harmless and juvenile. There is no way that one could have made anything out of it. He is saying whatever he is saying on his own. I didn't have anything to do with it."

"I…I don't understand. What did you tell him?"

"When he told me that he needed the room for tonight, because… you know… I just told him that yes, I knew what he meant!"

"And he thinks we did it based on that?"

"Yes! Which means he had been going around with this in his mind for almost forever. Right from the time you and I showed up at this door. And when I said that I knew what he meant, he thought that I was talking about the actual thing. About how it feels to have sex with you!"

Lizzy needed support. Her legs were giving way. She did not know which way to turn to. Here was a guy she had a one night stand with in a state of total drunken stupor, and on the other hand, outside somewhere, was her boyfriend of many years, who was perhaps going around with the thought that his girl had done it with someone else. It was true, yes, but how did it come into his mind?

Anurag could see her face change color. He knew that she didn't feel very bright inside. Even though his first reaction was that he had been successful, something else now took over his emotions completely. That of total sadness. She was his friend as well. A very good friend who had stood by him right from his first step on foreign soil. Even after all that had happened between them, she still had not left his side.

He crept forward towards her very slowly and, without any hesitation, drew her to himself, draped his hands around her. He could feel her shrink into his body, and then he felt a burning sensation around his neck. Then he felt something trickle down. She seemed to be unable to hold it in any longer. The pretense that her eyes were keeping for quite some time now broke down. And tears began to roll, like something was leaking inside.

Anurag could only hold her tighter and tighter in his arms. And he could feel her warm breath against his chin and neck. He could feel her arms tightening around him. And he could feel himself in love. He had never held a girl before in his life, but this was different than any feeling he had hoped to have. And when everything escapes logic and rationale, the answer is simple: love. The only logical scope to the whole thing.

Someone needed to say something. And sure as hell it was not going to be her. Even if she wanted to, she'd have no idea as to what to say. And when it is established that out of two people one won't speak, the other one has to be the one to start the dialogue. Or as it looked at that moment, a monologue.

"Lizzy, I think you should tell him…"

Silence.

"It really is the best thing to do. You don't want to live the rest of your lives doubting each other, do you?"

Silence. But it was the kind of silence that seems to offer a word. Something. To break the silence.

"Doubts? You think so? He thinks that I sleep with guys? He just thinks like that?"

Perhaps I should lighten the situation. I should make her smile. At least try to.

"Well, you did, you know!" he said and stroked his hand over her golden head and mocked laughter, more so to be heard than to actually mean it. It seemed to work, but only.

"I swear Anu, I have never slept with anyone apart from you. I have no idea what happened that night. Neither do you." She released her grip on him but not completely, she still stuck to him and used the sleeves of his sweater to wipe her face.

"You mean you don't just sleep with people?"

"No, never. Why would you even think that?"

"I don't know… Ronnie does. As does Sam and even Torrie. I thought it was pretty common with you Americans."

"I don't. I love him. Truly. He is everything to me. And even though I know that we did it that night, I had never thought that he feels that way. He didn't know; he shouldn't have thought!" And she fell into him again.

"Still… Talk to him. Get it out, and get it done with. Keeping it inside won't help."

"You're right. I think I will…"

"Do it now!"

She seemed to sense the tone. She pulled herself away from him and walked into the loo. She cleaned herself up and came back. There was a look of finality in her. She was going to make a decision. She was not going to just talk.

"I'll be back. Wait for me…" and she was gone. Anurag kept staring at the door for a long time after she'd left. He could still see her before him. Her hugging Lycra jeans, her disheveled striped sweater and her beautiful golden locks falling all over her face. Her image seemed real. He knew if he loved the impression, the impression of her in his mind, it might even reciprocate his love, even if the real being did not.

That was *the moment* of his life. Though even a kiss had not been exchanged, the feeling was orgasmic. And Anurag knew that he loved her more than ever.

Terms of Endearment

He must have been in his room for something like two hours, but it felt like an eternity. He had a project on small scale businesses in South East Asia to submit the next day, but he did not feel like going beyond his hole in the wall room for the requisite research. He just wanted some closure but perhaps that's not the right word, he just wanted to know what had happened between Aaron and Lizzy. He wanted their story to come to an end. He wanted Lizzy to be single again. For him to become her best friend, like he was a few hours back, consoling her, holding her, embracing her.

Now, he knew, may not be the best time to make a move, but Aaron's exit would be at least like half the battle won. And he could almost taste it, his half-victory. Actually, no. He couldn't taste anything and which was exactly the reason why he was almost panting with anxiety in his room, waiting for Lizzy to come back.

The clock ticked on and he could hear Big Ben chime courtesy the pin drop silence he was sitting in. The only other sound in the room was his own breath growing. And this sound was getting heavier with every passing second. And then suddenly, thanks to the silence, he heard the sound of footsteps growing louder. Whoever it was, he or she was either coming to him, or at least walking by. And there was every chance in the world that this person was Lizzy.

He dived back into his desk and flipped some pages of a book, pretending to be busy, with the eyes at the back of his head looking at the door. And it opened. It was the uglier half of Lizzy, Aaron, at the door. He did not look pissed, neither did he look pleased and this pissed off Anurag completely. *What on earth happened then? Did Lizzy not find him?*

It seemed that Aaron had not expected Anurag to be in the room. He was hoping to come back to an empty room, it was evident by the way he looked at him. It was like, "What the fu… oh! You here?" And Anurag too could not settle at an appropriate response. Should he be like "Oh you again?" or "Hey man!" or "I didn't do anything!" It was hard to fix his look.

But now that Aaron had seen him, it seemed that he had something to tell Anurag. After shifting in his place for quite some time, he slowly walked up to him. His swinging arms and confused eyes conveyed a lot even before he opened his mouth. Anurag was certain of one thing at least — that Aaron was not there to beat him up. So he rummaged through the thoughts running in his brain and came out with, "Hey man, what's up?"

"Uh, nothing to do with you bro, but Lizzy and I… well, let's just say that we are taking some time off from each other…"

"Huh?" *And I would like to thank the Academy for this award…*

"It's not been going well with us you know…"

"What?" *I would like to thank my parents, for sending me to America and making a man out of me…*

"Ya… It's not been the best… we were growing apart for quite some time now. And I really think this is the best thing for both of us…"

Anurag had run out of weird suitable expressions and weirder appropriate words to employ. So he just decided to adopt a bedazzled are-you-out-of-your-mind what-are-you-saying look for the time being.

"So, I'll be moving out of here for a while…"

This can't be happening. Way to go, Anurag! "But dude… How's that going to help?"

"Just that I need to be in a different place for a while… away from her. I'm leaving, going back to my folks for a while. I'll be like, returning next semester or something. I'm going to drop this semester."

"Hey, hey, hey! Dude, you can't do that… You need to go on studying. A girl can't make you go crazy in the head like that!" *OK, now I'm worried… what is this bozo talking about?*

"No, no… I'm not giving up studies man! Just taking some time off. It'll really help me focus for a while. Get myself back in the game completely."

"Well, if that's what it is… But I'm going to miss you man! You really helped me settle down here in the States. I couldn't have done it without you!"

"Hey no problem man! T'was all my pleasure… You go ahead with what you were doing, I'll just get my stuff together and be out of your hair!"

Aaron Reznor was going away. For a whole semester. To use his words again, he was really going to be out of Anurag's hair. Completely. Even his scalp it seemed. It was now that Anurag would actually start *living* in the States, it seemed. He was now in the state to be in the States: independent, and with a girl. He could surely get Lizzy, he knew it. He would, too.

Small scale businesses in South East Asia had never seemed so good before this. Everything was booming. The whole economy was booming. Anurag was booming. The whole god damned world was booming. Aaron Reznor was already boomed. This was the best report Anurag had ever worked on in all these months. He was going to bag his A effortlessly this time. He was the man!

Aaron took his time to get packed, mostly because he had a lot of junk sprawled all around the room. But soon it was time for him to go. After the customary handshakes and hugs, Aaron moved to the door. Anurag merely stood by his desk, waiting for him to go and yet feeling the feeling of loneliness sweep in slowly. He had offered to help, but Ronnie and Dustin had come to help Aaron move. All these chaps went to gym and it was surely going to be a whole lot easier for them to drag Aaron's bags.

Right at the door, the tall muscular defeated man turned around, and with his trademark smile, whispered, "See you later dude! Thanks for everything…" And then walked away. But, then he was back after five seconds, "Oh by the way… just before I leave, you want to get that game of squash?"

This had been going on forever now. Aaron had been pushing Anurag to come with him to the gym. But just the very idea of being surrounded in a room with people who all looked like Aaron was scary enough for him. There was no way in hell he was even planning to go anywhere near the gym. But the health freak in Aaron did not make do with a quitter answer. If not the gym, he had spent quite some time thinking up of all kinds of physical sports that Anurag could play to get into better shape. And finally, after a lot of pondering and debate, he had narrowed it down to squash. A quaint little sport; almost seemed like it was tailor made for Anurag.

Anurag had still been avoiding. Avoiding like hell. He just didn't think he was made out for any kind of physical activity. Surely his life had changed over the months. There was no doubt about that. He was not so much the guy who had come from India anymore. There were lesser communication breakdowns between him and Aaron and

Lizzy now; he got the basic concept behind what the other two spoke to him about, Yankee lingo and all. But still, a sport was hard work and not the kind of thing that he was personally interested in.

Anurag had been feeling pretty good about everything all this while, but these last few words squeezed and then pinched his heart. If Aaron had stayed there for even a couple of seconds more, he would have seen Anurag cry. Like a baby. "Thanks for everything", coming from such a huge muscular guy, in that tone, was just killing. It could have made even a man with a glass eye cry. It had said everything. And it had said it badly. Very badly. For the listener.

There seemed to be no way in which Anurag could say 'no' to him. It just did not seem possible one bit. It was like the last request of a man who was being sent to the gallows. And you always honor last wishes.

"Sure… when?"

"I'll be out of here in say around an hour or so… so, meet you at the complex in like, say, thirty?"

"I'll be there… but I don't have a racquet or anything… plus no protective gear! Where can I get that stuff?"

"I have an extra racquet, don't worry about that. And don't worry man… there is no protective gear necessary when playing squash. It's a pretty simple and easy game… you'll see!"

"Cool! I'll see you in thirty then!"

As soon as the door closed, Anurag sank into his seat

and cried his heart out on the table. To get a girl, he had humiliated another man, a person who had been nothing but nice to him ever since their first handshake. A person who perhaps always knew about everything that had happened that night, but not only did he never bring it to light, he also did not say anything to Anurag about it even after it was confirmed.

Anurag ambled to the Sports Complex. It was located at the other side of the campus and it was going to take him forever to get there. At least at the speed at which he was moving. While Aaron's words and his moving out had taking a toll on his feelings, he also wanted the entire process to end very soon. If Aaron was alright about leaving, then so be it. *He isn't going to give up studies, he is just putting some time between now and then. Perhaps that is a good thing,* thought Anurag as a friend.

Aaron was already there at the squash court. He was limbering up, something that Anurag had not even stopped to consider. Just shows that you are either a sports person, or you are not a sports person. Before Aaron handed him his gear, he made Anurag also go through all the required stretches and what have you. There was no way in which he'd led Anurag get hurt, it seemed. And all this was adding to Aaron's good books and was making Anurag more and more miserable. Soon they were ready to play.

Anurag had seen people play squash on TV. But he had no clue how the game was exactly played. All he knew was that there was a small ball that you have to keep hitting against the wall. And as far as common sense dictated, the task was to make it more and more difficult for your opponent to hit it back towards you. It seemed simple enough.

"Come on, I'll serve… you know the basic rules, right?"

"Don't worry, I'll figure it out as we go along! It's just hitting and returning, right?"

"More or less! Here, I'll go easy on you since this is your first time."

The words stung. True, Anurag had had never to do anything with sports ever, but being thought of and treated as some five year old child was pretty embarrassing for him. Even if there was no one else present there to hear that.

The serve was made, and Anurag smashed the ball as soon as he came somewhat close to it. And he hit it with such force that the ball ricocheted off the wall and came hurling back towards him. All this while Anurag had just thought that the ball was too small to cause any serious damage. But right then and there, seeing it hurtle towards him with bullet force, Anurag almost shat in his pants. Technically, Aaron was supposed to have hit it back, but Anurag had completely misplaced his shot — it was now coming directly back towards him. And there was no time for him to duck.

Anurag had almost mentally prepared himself to face the hard impact of the ball. But the hit never really came.

It seemed like an eternity since Anurag had crouched to assume his hunched position. His feet had stopped. There was no blood left in them to go anywhere. But he kept just standing there in one position for what seemed like forever. Nothing happened.

Anurag finally opened his eyes once again. It wasn't possible for the ball to take that long to come back and strike him. And strike him dead at that. But he was still breathing. And not even feeling any pain. However, he could see nothing in front of him. It was a complete black out. Had he been hit dead by the ball? And were these the gates to heaven or hell? Was this what people called a painless death? It was still completely dark all around him. There was nothing to see. He was dead.

"Hey man, you alright?"

Aaron was dead too! I killed him too! I am a murderer. No, I 'was' a murderer.

"Dude, get up man!"

Anurag was still trying to feel his surroundings. It was strange to him. Or so he at least thought. Very slowly, the blur started lifting. More and more of the surroundings flooded into Anurag's vision. He was apparently still on planet earth. His heart was still pumping extra gallons of blood through his system. His breathing had gone haywire, but his lungs were still functioning. And yet there was no inclination of pain anywhere in his system.

It was strange. It was something that he couldn't explain. Aaron was right there in front of him. He had the ball in his hand, but his other hand was stroking his own chest. *What the hell happened here?*

"Dude, you ok?" Aaron was still asking the same question. Naturally, his question had not been answered till then.

"Yes, I think so... but what happened? Wasn't that ball coming right at me?"

"You hit it too hard man! And not in the right direction either. You didn't have enough time to duck, so I covered you. No biggie."

Aaron had taken the blow himself. He had saved Anurag from a lot of pain. A whole lot of pain. Anurag didn't quite know what to say, do or even think. Here he was, screwing around with this man, making his life miserable, and taking pleasure from doing all this, and this guy was still watching his back — just like he had promised that day at Taj Mahal.

"Dude, I'm pretty wasted with that blow... mind if we take this game on to some other day?"

"Sure! Thanks so much bro... that really was something!"

"Hey, don't mention it... what are brothers for!"

His smile was a little rickety, but the assurance was still there. "See ya around man!" And after a hug, Aaron walked away, still trying to grease his chest free from the pain. Anurag felt a tear trickling down his face.

As he wiped his tears from his choked face, Anurag wondered if he would have felt better if Aaron had just punched and left him with a black eye. Non-violence hurts worse -- he became convinced of this that day. Aaron Reznor was the better man, surely. No one could debate this fact. He had belted Anurag without even lifting a muscle.

But it was time to move on. And make a move. Surprisingly, Anurag had no intention of making Lizzy a believer in his love for her and all that jazz at that moment. Right then, all he wanted to do was to go and stand by her, be there for her. If Aaron had taken it this badly, then she must have completely crumbled. She must need him then. She must need her friend. And whichever way it were to turn out, he decided he was going to act like a true friend in that moment of severe need.

His report done, Anurag ran from there. He had to find her, wherever she was.

Lightning Always Strikes Twice

She was nowhere where he had expected her. He wasn't even able to reach her through phone. Anurag searched the entire campus over and over again. But she was nowhere to be found. He tried all the places he knew she went to, even tried the places where her friends hung out. She wasn't there either. He even went down to Taj Mahal, the restaurant, but she wasn't there too.

He was starting to get worried. Lizzy, underneath her bold, carefree exterior was really a child and Anurag knew that. She was the girl he was in love with, and therefore he knew everything about her. Hence, he was not ruling out the possibility of her ending up doing something stupid. She was vulnerable then, and liable to do anything and everything stupid under the sun. Aaron's condition was warning enough for Anurag to become gravely worried about her.

Tensed, fed up and worried, Anurag knew he'd had have to go into the city to find her. He had established without doubt that she was not in the campus. He needed to carry some money for that, and so he ran back to his room. He would just collect his wallet and run off. He had no clue where to find her, but he'd roam through the whole of Rochester if required.

But as soon as he walked into his room, he was relieved. She was in his room. She had been sitting there for him, all this while. She had come to him, completely broken. Her look said it all. The possibility of Aaron leaving her, or even either of them leaving the other, had been completely absent from her calculations. And now that it had happened, she was left completely dazed, confused, bitter and what not. She had gone out of his room to talk to Aaron some three hours back, but the person who was now sitting in his room, on his bed was someone far different. She looked nothing like her usual self — it was really that bad.

"He's... gone!"

Just those two words said it all. He knew it, he knew that he was gone – Aaron had walked out of his room just an hour back, but it sunk in completely only now that she voiced it. Because what she had voiced were not just a couple of words put together, it was a complete void. She was empty from within. And she sounded every bit of it.

He walked over to her. She was sitting facing the door. She was waiting for him to come back. He could make it out. He knew it. It was written all over. It seemed strange to Anurag as to what love can do to a person. It seemed worse than every other human tragedy that the human mind is capable of churning up.

He sat down beside her, took her hands in his and gave a half smile, which actually couldn't be categorized as a smile to begin with.

"I know... he was here. He told me!"

Lizzy jumped up immediately, her eyes looking for some hope. "He was here? What did he say? Do you know where he went?"

"He didn't tell you?"

"No... we didn't get that far... where is he? I need to go and talk to him!"

"What do you want to tell him?"

"I don't know... I don't want him to go. I can't live without him."

"Lizzy, it's over. You know that as much as I do... Just let it go."

"No, no, no... it's not over. It can't be. It's just a misunderstanding, it will be fine. I must talk to him."

"He's gone Lizzy. He put this distance between the two of you on his own. Maybe he thinks that's the best way to go about it. And perhaps you should too."

She was broken completely. She was behaving like a person who was going through a nervous breakdown. She was shaking. Trembling all over. She had no idea of what to do. Perhaps she had come here to stop Aaron. Maybe to tell him that she loved him. But she was too late. And he was gone. Anurag undoubtedly felt miserable for her, but he was also happy as he needed that distance between the two of them for his own love story to work. He needed to get her over him. Fast.

"Lizzy, tell me something. Was he the first guy you fell in love with?"

Unable to speak, she merely nodded, a very faint and distant nod. It was more like a reflex answer to that question.

"Maybe that's why it's so hard. You never saw anything beyond Aaron. But there is a whole world still open to you. The first cut is the deepest, I agree. But then every wound heals. And this will too. You just need to give it time."

"But I had planned out my whole life with him. How can it end like this?"

"Oh come on! Life never goes according to a 'plan', does it? It doesn't and you should know that. We all hope for stuff and then when it does not happen, we have to make other plans to mitigate the pain of failure. Life has to go on. It hurts, it makes you wish you weren't alive anymore, but you still need to go about it somehow. Just because one plan did not work, that does not mean it's the end of everything!"

She looked up at him. Her blue eyes quivered as they looked at him. The tears that had rolled down had now dried up, leaving a patchy effect over her white cheeks. All color had been drained from her face. She was looking like a zombie now. She knew that he was saying the right thing but she did not want to hear it then. That's exactly the trouble with truth — it is never something you want to hear.

"Lizzy, not that I want to take away anything from your grief right now and neither am I implying anything, but that night, whatever you may want to call it that happened between us, I made some plans. And believe me, I had been making those plans right through the day. Love at first sight exists and you know that. And yet, the next morning in the train, right to this day, those plans just washed themselves away. And here I still am, trying to make you feel better. You have to get over it!"

She listened to him. Rather intently. But leaving a huge, warm, dry breath, she asked, "Have you been able to get over me then?"

She had played him in. He was now surrounded by the Wizard's legions and he had nowhere to go. And the old adage, that when you cannot find your way out of a mess, the best thing is to go deeper into it. Perhaps you'd find a way out somewhere. He must say something to balance out all ends. He must play this very carefully. It took all of his sharp intelligence to come up with something appropriate to play this question.

"No, I did not. And believe me, I never will. But then I had to make a choice. Give you up completely because you were with someone else, or still be with the only friend that I had in America, the only one person that I could actually call a friend. It was a change in plans. I had to make it. But then, the latter was the new plan. You aren't with me, and I don't know if you ever will be, but at least at this moment, when you need someone, I am there with you. That means a lot to me and I can live with it."

Touché!

Her eyes dropped back once again. She had been defeated. But, more importantly, she understood the point he was trying to make. She would have to move on. Think of life without Aaron. And the sooner she did it the better. She didn't want to see the outside world till then. She would get back her life before she leaves this room. She made a decision.

"You have any of that Bacardi I had left here last time?"

"I think it should be here somewhere… Why?"

"I agree with you… I need to get over him. And you and I need to celebrate. To my being single again, and to us being friends forever. At least that. So, open the bottle and let us drink a toast to ourselves and our lives."

"You and I, drinking? Is that such a good idea?" He was concerned, sure, about the repercussions that could follow from the two of them drinking again, but then, what she wanted was more essential then. So after his question, he added a small, fluctuating wink to punctuate her response, to get her to laugh, to get her to smile again at least. He had also not missed out on a key phrase she had uttered: *"…to us being friends forever. At least that."* There was hope, there was a lot of hope.

"Ah, screw it. This time, there won't be any guilt feelings." And she burst out laughing. It was the same laugh he had heard on his first day in America. It had that same twinkling feel to it, that same jittery expression. He knew she was back to the moment of their first meeting. She was no longer Elizabeth Morgan. She was once again Dizzy Miss Lizzy.

They drank through the night. When he got up the next morning, he felt like someone had tied Aaron's dumbbells to his brain. It was about to explode. Even as he got his bearings back to reality, he saw Lizzy sleeping right next to him. Something felt funny. There was something missing from the whole picture.

Petrified that lightning had struck again at the same place, he rushed to the loo. And yes, it was there in the commode. He and her, they had done it again! It was no longer a mistake then. It had happened twice now. She wouldn't be able to back out of it anymore. It was done. He and she were together now. By the bonds of bodily fluids and pharma company condom rates, they had been pronounced boyfriend and girlfriend. She still had to say "I do", but the very fact that they were at the altar before the priest was good enough for him.

The last time he had been in the loo, he had been shaking shitless. This time too he was shaking shitless, but it was feeling better. Much, much, much better.

You Make Me Dizzy
Miss Lizzy

By the time she got up, Anurag had already got some coffee and muffins ready for her. Once again, she frantically started searching for something around the bed as soon as she got up. Only this time Anurag was sitting right next to her, with the bra in his hand.

"It was lying there, on the floor. Must have fallen off!"

She extended her hand and took it from him, but she didn't look at him directly. Rather, a coy smile was all that he got. It was almost routine now. Drink with Anurag and wake up next morning without your clothes on! But this time there weren't really any guilt feelings. There was no Aaron to think about. There was no nothing to think about. The benefits of being single.

"Coffee?"

He had made coffee for her. He had a muffin along with it too. Aaron never did that. Ever. He had surely taken her for granted. He had convinced himself that she would never leave him and, somehow, he had even managed to convince her about the same. But that was not to be. Love cannot run on tales and make-believe. And she knew that now.

"What happened last night?" she ventured to ask, knowing full well. But it was worth a conversation starter. She had placed her bra back on, but it was pointless trying to hide away from Anurag. Clearly he might not remember, but he had surely had an acid rock fest over her the night before. And of course vice versa. She just wrapped the blanket around her and sat there, sipping the dark liquid.

"The usual... too much booze!" and he smiled back at her. It was becoming a habit now!

"Either we stop drinking... or we stop sleeping. But I guess it's interlinked." And she raised her hands up in the air.

"The only problem is that I never get to know whether I was any good or not! You remember anything?"

"Nopes! Not one thing... it's like it's a blank place somewhere in time. You just go there but then everything stands still!"

As the little jitter escaped from his lips, he almost choked on his muffin. "Nothing stands still. I am pretty sure of that at least!"

And they both shared a laugh. Their first. "So, what have you got for today?"

"I have some classes. A paper to submit. Then I

promised to go to that DVD place that Torrie works at. She was telling me that they were looking for someone to work there. And I thought I might do it. Will get me some money to spare."

"Ah nice! And now you'll have someone to spend it on."

Choke. Muffin. Breathless. Sweaty. It all happened together. She had said it. He thought he didn't hear it right. It couldn't have been the way he heard it. Not now. Not so soon. He had to get some kind of clarification from her. He just had to.

"Huh?" *Sorry Lizzy baby, but that's all that's going to come out.*

"You know… it's a good thing that you'd be earning some money now. Coz, then you'd be able to spend it on me. I am kind of high maintenance you know!"

"Yes… sure… I… but… then… you…"

"The stutter is back, is it?"

"Yes… you… know… what…" *Oxygen, oxygen, someone cut it off. Damn it!*

"Yes!"

"Y...e...s…?"

"That's a new best… stuttering within the same word. You've never done that before!"

"Then… You… I…"

"Yes!" and then she sealed it. She let the blanket drop. And he had his first, conscious look at her brassier-covered breasts. He was about to faint. And then, she swooped right before him and for the first time that he was aware of, she pressed her lips on his. He was powered back to life, as his own lips started moving. And his hands pressed her towards him, closer and closer, till he could feel her all over him. Now, this was a feeling that he had never experienced. Unlike anything, and that included the first time he had slept with her.

When he had gone to sleep the night before, whenever it might have been, he had never expected to get up to this day. After the day when he had first stepped foot on America, this was the greatest day of his whole life. He was finally with a striker of a girl, the girl of his very dreams, his best friend. She was the first American friend he had ever had. And now she was also his girlfriend. It could've never gotten better than this.

She left soon after, promising to be back in the evening once he was back from 'work'. He got dressed and went for classes. Professor Freeman's class on market dynamics never seemed so good. He could absorb everything like a sponge. He submitted his paper and ran off to the city, to Al's DVDs. Torrie was already there and she took him on board with a smile on her lips.

Everything went ahead like clockwork. Everything fit in very well with everything that day. The day on which he shared his first conscious kiss with Lizzy. The day his love had won. The day he had won. As he sorted out the DVDs and placed them in the right shelves, he couldn't help but look back at the young Anurag in school. The one who had been scared to death when Alisha Mahapatra had walked over to him and… that was it, 'walked up to him'. And look at that same Anurag now. The decision he had made thereafter, after having been left bruised and battered both outside and inside, to come to America to study had paid off in spades — not only had he got the scholarship, Anurag Sinha had also become a human being. A man. In the true sense of the word. A man who fought for his girl. He was John Wayne. A cowboy.

In all the time that he had stayed in America, Anurag had never wanted to go back to his room — which was why it was easier to find him in the library. But today he could just not wait to get back to his room. Every minute organizing *Citizen Kane* and *The Clockwork Orange* was killing him. He knew one thing for sure: that the minute his shift comes to an end, he was going to make a new record of sprinting back the fastest from Main Street to the campus.

Five more minutes to go, exactly, by the clock, and the miraculous happened. His phone buzzed in his pants, vibrating everything there. Holding a worn out copy of *Once Upon a Time in the West*, Anurag fished out his cell. He had just received a message.

Cum fast. Ur room. Surprise.

It was from Lizzy. She had sent out a moose call to her man. She was calling him back. The mother ship was calling him in. And how could he wait? Work never felt so boring. And he never felt so impatient ever. The three minutes left on the giant clock across the door were the longest he had ever spent. He cleared the balance tapes in record time and then with just one minute left to tick over, he started getting himself ready for takeoff.

The traffic that evening was bad. It had to be, or else old man Murphy would be out of a job. But how does it matter to a man on foot what song the cars were singing that day. In Hollywood*ish* style, Anurag leaped across the boots of many cars and kept running. Not even once did he feel the nagging pain in his knees and soles. He didn't stop. For anything.

He rushed through the main gate of the campus and kept running still, till he reached his room door. Owing to Newton's laws of rest and motion and all that jazz, he was unable to stop himself even as he crashed right through the door and skidded inside uncontrollably.

When he now stopped, gasping for breath, he saw what the surprise was. She was there, inside, waiting for him like she had promised. And she had cooked. Food. For the two of them. The lights were all off and there were candles everywhere. This was the surprise.

Prior to Lizzy, Anurag had no idea as to what love was. But now he realized that just sleeping together or the fact that Lizzy was the only girl who he could talk to easily were not the mere constituents of the thing called love. The fact that he just ran nonstop for almost an eternity after frantically waiting for his working hours to get over, and the fact that she had gone through all the trouble to do all this for him… *this is love. It is this feeling that people refer to as love.*

Lizzy was wearing her trademark jeans, sneakers and one of her black shirts, and in the candlelight she looked like an angel, but surely was the devil in disguise. He could see the light and dark patches on her golden tresses, and how even though she had tied them at the end, several locks had escaped the band and were now flying over her face. Her cheeks were glowing red and she just stood there before him, transfixed.

"Surprised?"

"(puff) Ye…(pant)...ah! To…(puff)...tall…(pant)…y!"

"Jesus! What happened to you?"

"I… just ran…all the way…"

"What?" and she giggled that giggle again, killing him with every spurt of it.

"Yeah, couldn't wait...to see you…"

Her eyes swelled, and her lips creased her face. She liked it, that much was obvious. She liked the fact that he took that effort for her.

"You know, Aaron was the gym guy and he never even walked fast enough for me… Interesting, isn't it, how much you know about a person after his back is turned on you?"

Crisis. Aaron time.

"It's quite the other way around actually… you turned your back on him! So… let him learn more stuff about you, and let us eat this awesome dinner you made… you know, before it gets cold!"

She gave him that 'clever bugger' look. She knew what he was doing. And there was every possibility, as made evident in the way she looked at him, that she liked it. He pulled himself to the desk which was now serving as the table and plopped himself down on it. Like the quintessential Indian wife, she made sure he was served first and as he took the first bite, she stared at him, biting her lip and nails at the same time. Even if the food had tasted terrible, looking at her give that look, he would never have been able to say anything to the purpose.

But it did not taste anything but divine. So much so that the thought crossed his mind that she might have got the food from outside. She had not. The number of bottle of herbs and other such crap on the table told him that she had made it on the electric stove that Aaron had forgotten to carry back with him.

"You did this for me?"

"Yup!" Her nervousness had eased up a bit. She was just biting her lip now as her hand took its place by the platform, supporting his frame. "Like it?"

"It's out of the world… no one ever did that for me before!"

"I had done it for Aaron too…"

Again. "Don't we drink some wine shine along with this?"

"Not tonight!"

"He he he he! I see… not tonight!" and he made those big eyes that are supposed to make the point without actually saying it. And he turned back to sip his water.

And then, suddenly, before he even knew it, she bent

down and crossed her arms around him, running her nose all over his ear. He just froze with that glass at his lips. She, on the other hand, kept snuggling. Her hands kept wandering over his chest, as her lips caressed the sides of his head. Before he could, she used her hand to shoo away the glass and turned his head towards her and placed her lips on his.

It was the best kiss of his life. Sensuous, full, warm. Reflexes took over, and he closed his arms around her, holding her closer and closer to himself. His hands rubbed all over her back, as their tongues dove deeper and deeper into their mouths. As she pulled her head lose, and it was only for a momentary pause, she whispered in his ears, "Today we do it without getting drunk… so that we know what we are doing!"

Anurag was feeling it for the first time, as his thing started to climb up. He was moving completely on his own now, and slowly, he used all his strength to push the two of them away from the table. The small little jerk that they gave in doing so, doused the last candle on the table. Perfect timing.

When Anurag Sinha got up the next morning, everything felt different. He was finally living the life he had dreamt of. Always. And which had intensified after their first meeting at Grand Central. He didn't get up and run to the loo that day. He had nothing to check. He knew what all had happened the night before. This morning, all he could do, and all he wanted to do, was just sit there and look at her sleeping. He didn't mind if she never woke up — not in the dead sense — he would just keep sitting there forever, looking at her. Till the time he died, surely.

Who's the man?
He's the man!

The only thing that Anurag kept telling himself in the coming months was that he could get used to living like this. Life was a melody. Lizzy was there, he was there, everything else was not there and neither was it needed. Several months passed by. Anurag grew stronger and stronger in his studies, being so much more able to concentrate on his school work now. His work at the DVD parlor was monotonous and boring and well below his skill grade, but it didn't matter. For the money he made there was more than enough to show Lizzy a good time. And for Anurag, that was all that mattered.

America was cheap. Sure, the amount he made working at the Al's was like peanuts, but considering the fact that the dollar bought so much more, he could save enough in a few years to perhaps buy a house. The economics classes sure were coming in handy somehow or the other. Now was that time that the Customs official had perhaps told him about when he had landed in JFK. It was that time when every immigrant into America starts wondering: what next? Should I stay here? Should I go back? And more often than not, the answers were answered even before the questions popped up.

For Anurag, it was not just the financial gain at the end of it. It was the emotional one as well. Now, he realized he wouldn't be able to survive without Lizzy. And that meant staying here. Why on earth would she even contemplate leaving the comforts of America and going to the dingy mess of India? Sure, it was home and all and all that jazz, but then, it was the choice between a certain posh way of life, against another posh way of life, only that the latter was posh just on the surface. Living in America, fitting in amongst her people, Anurag had easily made that demarcation between his adopted nation and his birth country. It was perhaps because of this that Anurag had finally become more than a wimpy goofy kid.

The only thing that bothered him, truthfully, was the fact that she kept referring Aaron like a cross index from time to time. But with time he came to accept the fact that try what he did, Aaron would not go out of Lizzy's mind. Not for a long time, if not forever.

It was almost the end of the last semester. The finals were approaching fast. And Anurag, who had by now saved a lot of money, had given up working, substituting that instead with studying. His parents had sacrificed a lot to send him here, the scholarship aside, and he owed it to them to get good grades.

And it was then, one fine day, that he felt a hand slip on his shoulder while he was slogging over mostly every book he could find in the library.

"Hey bro! Long time…"

That voice. That very same voice. The one that he dreaded. He was back.

Gingerly, Anurag turned his books around on the table and peered back to see if his worst dream had come true. And it had. How could it not? We are talking about Anurag, the man with the bad luck!

"Hey man… been a while now, hasn't it?" Aaron Reznor was standing right behind him. Anurag felt himself break into cold sweat right then and there. It had really been a long time since the day Aaron had said those killing words and moved out. And as he and Lizzy had come closer, he had completely forgotten that Aaron would return. Like he was gone forever. But here he was today, back, right in front of him.

But it was not the same man that he knew. Aaron Reznor was now just a cheap copy of himself. He had lost all his looks, his physique — so much so, he even looked shorter now. He initially knew it was Aaron no doubt, but when he kept looking at him for some seconds, Anurag wondered whether he really was his ex-roomie and ex-boyfriend of his girlfriend.

"Aaron?" He couldn't help but just ask. He needed some confirmation.

"Ya man! I knew I'd find you here in the library. It's just been so long. Thought I'd come and give you a look see!"

And Aaron, or rather Aaron the Lionhearted, closed his lanky hands around Anurag and gave him a best friends' hug. Anurag still could not believe what he was seeing. Or feeling. Aaron was strengthless.

"Good to see you buddy! But what on earth happened? You look… like horrible man!"

"Honesty has been your song man!" and Aaron smiled at him. "I'm working on it. I'll be back to usual soon enough dude! How's it going with you?"

"Seriously man… you just have to… I'm doing good. Semester exams and all, so studies. Where were you all these days?"

"Great man! I went back home… did some small jobs I could find. But I'm back now. And I think the whole break helped. Like a lot!"

"So, you over her now?" This was it. The most important question, one that Anurag had actually wanted to be the first question in this whole conversation.

"No. I guess that will never happen. But I fouled up and paid the price. So I guess I'll just have to live with that…"

"You really loved her that much then?"

"Sure did… but let's forget that now. Ronnie tells me

you two are a pair now. I'm happy for you bro. She couldn't have got a better guy. I'd always wish that, if not me, she is with someone like you. Someone who'll love and care for her!"

"Hmmm!" *Words, Aaron. Words.*

"So anyways… I'll take off now. Come over some day. I'm shacking up with Dennis now and we'll have a small little party of our own!"

"Sure man… We'll make a plan. I'll come over!"

"Do that… see ya!"

And Aaron walked away. Just the sight of him could kill someone. He looked like the perfect case for malnutrition, shrunk to his very bones. He had not taken the break well, whatever he might say against that. It was visible. It was literally visible.

Anurag's mind was completely off studies now. Only Aaron and his words reverberated inside his head. He knew it was pointless looking at the books now. So he packed up, left the library and headed back to his room. He needed to relax. A healthy, happy Aaron would not have bothered him. This version did.

As he turned the knob of his door and moved in, he found Lizzy already there, doing some studies of her own. Even she was to be tested, to be told whether she was any good at her musicology or not.

"Hey honey! You came back rather early!"

"Uh huh! Just couldn't concentrate… I think I have a headache coming!"

"You're working too hard... just take a break... Lie down here!"

"Ya..."

And Anurag collapsed on his side of the bed. She was still lying on her stomach, pouring over her books, but her gaze was turned backwards, towards Anurag. She peered at him over her glasses, as if trying to see how sick he really was. As in whether he needed any medical attention or not.

But for the first time in all the times they had been together, Anurag was not looking at her. He just lay there, his eyes resting squarely on the ceiling. He could just see Aaron there. The 'new' and surely not improved Aaron Reznor. He had read of love killing people slowly, but this was something else. Anurag was scared that something might happen to him.

And yet on the other hand was Lizzy. His first, and preferably last love. She was with him. She was his. He was hers. There was no way in which that equation was going to be messed up. Not for Aaron, not for anyone.

And why should it even be any kind of an issue? She was over him, even if he was not. Once he saw that perhaps he'd know that his time was up. And he'd get that much-needed closure that he was probably looking for. That was it then. That was all that was required in his case. As for her, the case was already closed. She was with him and she was happy and content.

"You really look worried... Is something the matter?"

"Huh?" He was lost. Way lost. He had no idea where he was, or for that matter, the fact that she was also there with him. And he was so completely entangled in his own mental monologues that he had not heard her.

"Is everything alright, Anu? You…seem weird today."

Of course she was right. He was anything but normal. "No, nothing much actually. Just overworked I guess."

"Alright… I guess… But be careful. Aaron got a huge burn out when he was trying out for the football team. Had the same problems!"

Aaron. Again!

To Think Of It

She had said it again. And to think of it, she used it pretty much often during a whole day. It was like a punctuation in her sentences. Sometimes, it started a conversation, at other times, it ended one. And though it was something that he had made his peace with, that day, the story was completely different.

He must get to the bottom of this. He had to know where he stood. And he also knew that he did not want to end up at the wrong end of this story. He couldn't afford to now that he had seen the physical proof of the result of ending up at the wrong end of this stick. He had seen Aaron in flesh and blood, or rather without much of either. No longer was the forlorn lover a character in books. It was a fact. A known fact. A very well known fact. And under no circumstances did he want to be one such.

But he wasn't going to become an ostrich. He couldn't just put his head under the sand and think that the problem was gone. Whoosh! He had to face it. He didn't want to, but then again, who likes facing the truth? He had to bite the bullet and the sooner he was killed, the sooner his doubts would come to an end. Death frees everyone.

"Lizzy, can I ask you something?"

"Yeah! Sure…"

"Aaron… he's not out of your mind completely even now, is he?"

She had not been looking at him then. She was working on something, taking down some notes, leafing through some pages. But now she stopped. She stopped with a jolt. Not a pleasant sight for a loving boyfriend wondering whether he's going to be pushed off the edge or not.

"What?"

"Just a question… Nothing more than that!"

"Where did that come from?"

"I just asked it… it's not a biggie. Just tell me… have you been able to get over him completely?"

"Why are you even asking this?"

"Please Lizzy… I need to know this… Are you over him?"

"I can't believe you are actually asking this…"

"And I can't believe that you are actually not answering the question!"

She paused. She stopped completely then and looked at him. And kept looking at him. Transfixed.

He saw her look depraved. He saw the look she gave him. And he knew the answer. She was caught. And she knew it. And therefore the look was all that she could give. She couldn't speak to him and confirm the obvious. Not to him.

"Am I right?"

She still didn't answer. She just kept looking. As if that would make time go away. As if that would make this moment change. But it didn't. Only that the loud silence amplified the moment and the stark reality that it was trying to hide. It didn't matter what she said now. Her look had secured her answer.

"I am right!"

Naturally, no response.

"Lizzy, couldn't you have just told me?"

"What could I tell you? What was there to tell?" Tears welled up around the corners of her eyes. She was fighting them. Had been fighting them for quite some time now.

"Just be honest with me... It's been quite some time now that we've been together. All I could expect was that you'd come and tell me if something was bothering you!"

"Really? Tell you that Aaron is not out of my mind? Or tell you that even after everything, even though I know that you are the most understanding and loving man that I'd ever have in my whole life, all I think about the whole day is Aaron! How on earth do you think I could tell you that?"

"If I really am that caring and understanding, don't you think I would have understood?"

"Even then... you don't say these things. You just don't. I thought I'd forget about him over time. But it just did not happen that way. It just didn't. He remained in my head, tucked away somewhere. And he did not go..." She was howling now. All that she had managed to keep within her for the past one and a half years was now coming out. In full force. A gate had been opened. It was a dam breaking free. And it was some kind of relief. Relief that she would not have to live a pretense any more.

And not for the first time in his life, Anurag was at a crossroads of what should be done and what needn't been done. Only this time, the choice was as personal as it could get. There was Lizzy on both sides — a Lizzy for him and a Lizzy for Lizzy. And somehow it was the first one that came to his mind instantaneously. Perhaps she was right. It needed time. Lots of time. And she'd get over Aaron. Surely.

"And every time I wanted to see him, just look at him, hear him speak... I couldn't do anything about it because I never knew where he was, or what he was doing, or whether he was even alive or dead! And therefore I kept trying to push it away from myself. Each and every day. But, Anu, even though I still love him, believe me, I say this with all honesty, he was nothing and totally nothing when compared to you..." and she kept howling. Thundering now.

Anurag lifted his head from his hands, where he had buried it a moment back. He was better than Aaron. He knew when she was being honest. And this was not only her being honest, this was the moment of truth too. The truth that she had digested and stored away inside herself. Today it was pouring out and she was not adding spices just to notch up the taste of the tale. That day, after a long long time, she actually meant each and every word that she was saying.

"Lizzy, I understand…"

"How can you? How can you understand that I'm such an awful girl... telling the best friend she ever had, the best lover she ever had that she still cares about the idiot she had before him? How can you?"

"I still can… because the best friend you ever had is still very much your best friend and will remain to do so. And he can always understand what you are going through."

She stopped choking, and looked at him. His words were actually reaching her. He was saying it. Slowly, gently.

"I always knew that Aaron was tucked away somewhere in your mind… after all, you spoke about him like a hundred times a day, each and every day! But I had made my peace with that… I think you needed to have this out in the open. Perhaps get some closure, so that it helped…"

"Anu, stop…" She had to get it out now, now that everything was out there on the table. "I may have whatever I have for this guy. I may love him, hate him, remember him, anything. But the fact of the matter is that he's doing fine without me… He is out there, somewhere and most probably I am just a forgotten chapter in his life now. And, no sir, I am not going to deal with that. I have my bloody closure and this has served me well enough!"

Anurag felt breathless. As if something dreadful had happened there. As if someone had murdered him in cold blood.

"Is that all you are basing your closure on?"

"Doesn't it look like reason enough to you?"

Yes, she was.

Anurag very slowly rose from his bed and stood there, his hands running over his mouth to try and jolt him out to some conclusion. But one thing he knew, anyone else in his position would have also known it: this was all wrong. She was doing what he had wanted her to do, but she was doing it wrong. It was unjustified, it was a mistake.

Lizzy kept starting at him, her face once again left blazing by the dried tears. She had thought he would show a more relieved expression than the one he was showing right then on hearing the truth. But he was now more perturbed than usual. And it was not right.

"What's wrong?"

He stopped and looked at her. And her look, those innocent, flashing, large eyes, they said it all. He walked towards her and sat down right next to her. He took her hands in his, treasuring the moment.

"Lizzy, if I didn't know better, I'd say he's dying without you!"

Her hands had been loose till then but suddenly they became stiff. "What?"

"Yes... I saw him. And he looks like a bigger wimp than me now."

Lizzy froze. She looked at him, her eyes ready for a second burst now.

"Lizzy, Aaron is not the same guy anymore. And he can't accept the fact that you two are not together anymore. He just can't. All that he can think of is you. He went home, worked as a plumber, carpenter, waiter, anything he could lay his hands on to get some distance between you two. But it didn't work..."

Right at that moment, Lizzy found out what true love was. That Aaron cared. That he had not just left her for good. He wasn't cozying up next to the next bimbette that walked into the room.

"He still loves me?"

"More than ever. And I think you should go to him..."

"Where did you see him?"

"Run down the hall. Dennis's room. He's there..."

She broke her hands away from his and leapt out of the bed. She somehow managed to dig her feet into her shoes and jump to the door. But then she stopped as her hand reached out for the knob and turned back.

"Anu... you?"

"I wouldn't live a single minute more knowing that you and Aaron could not be together because of me... I love you too much for that... I'll be ok. Get along now!"

Her voice choked as she spoke. "Aaron can never replace you… ever… no one can!"

"I know…" and he smiled at her and she was gone.

EPILOGUE

Grand Central was buzzing as usual. And Anurag thought that perhaps there was never a time when the station did not horn its way to glory. As he got off the train from Rochester, pulling his luggage with him, he stopped to remember his last few memories at the University.

Graduation day. Being the topper. Again. And finally, his talk with Lizzy.

"So, Mr. Tops, what's going to happen now?"

"Just so that you know, there is a company called Tops which makes ketchup back at home… so… But to answer your question, I'm going home!"

Her jaw dropped. "What? How can you go home? How? You have to stay here!"

"I don't quite want to raise this issue again… so just buy what I'm saying."

"Oh don't say that you are going back because of me…"

"Aaron went home when you broke up with him... I, by my own admission love you about ten times more... so not only do I have to go back home, I have to put that much distance between the two of us too. Luckily, my home is just that far!"

"What will I do if you go away?"

"Concentrate on everything around here... especially on Aaron. He looks better than that haunted house expose he gave me at the library that day, but still... he has miles to go to look like his old self again. Don't worry, we'll be in touch. And maybe, this time for a change, you can come to meet me!"

Even though they were standing right before each other, she ran to hug him, knocking the air out of him completely. And they stayed there forever, time going berserk, unable to move forward.

Now, at Grand Central, as he walked past the phone booths, he saw that day vividly again. And he walked up to the same phone booth he had used to call his mother, next to the one where she was standing, hearing in on the conversation. And he felt the timeline of his life only going forward from that point on.

He stood there as he realized what America had done for him. America had turned a shy, introvert boy who couldn't talk to girls into a man. A man who believed in what was right, who didn't back away from fighting for his girl, but who also didn't back out from letting her get what she wanted. When he had come to America he had not much personality to speak of but now he was going back as a rock solid man. He could now speak, he could now talk, he could now act, he could now behave. And he was a whiz with girls. If only he could meet Alisha Mahapatra now. Would be fun.

He somehow managed to carry himself down to the central entrance and waved out for a cab. After putting all his luggage in the boot and in the back seat, he finally sat down in a NYC cab again to go towards JFK. He looked at the driver's ID and it read Dmitri Shkel. *Dmitri Shkel?* The same cabbie who had not charged him his fare from JFK to Central! His first friend…

"Hi! Remember me pal?"

"Ekskuze meeh?"

"Dmitri… Anurag… you brought me to Grand Central from JFK some two years back… you didn't charge me my fare since it was my first time in your country… remember?"

"Ah! Muh Eendiaan frend… hou aarrrr yoh?"

He was now waiting for his boarding call. America. Will be missed. Lizzy more so. He had never known love like that. And maybe he never would. Very honestly, she chose a second option. Maybe he'd have to do the same. Just as he sipped his coffee, his phone beeped. It was a text.

I'll always love you, my friend. Always. Even in my last hour, I will think of you and you only. Travel safe!

Lizzy must have meant it. No shorthand. She had

taken the trouble to write proper English. Anurag smiled. And quickly hit the reply button.

Since the time I saw you, you have never left my mind. And till my last second, you'd always be in my heart. One life, one love. And her name shall always be Lizzy. See you.

He tried to crowd his mind as tears welled up behind his eyes. His family was coming to receive him at IGI. The whole family. Three Innovas. They'd bring flowers. A mess at IGI. Again.

Dmitri, Grand Central please… On the double!!